Johns Hopkins: Poetry and Fiction
John T. Irwin, General Editor

Fiction Titles in the Series

Safety Patrol

Short Stories by

MICHAEL MARTONE

The Johns Hopkins University Press
Baltimore & London

10/1988
am Lit

This book has been brought to publication with the generous assistance of the G. Harry Pouder Fund and the Albert Dowling Trust.

The Johns Hopkins University Press
701 West 40th Street
Baltimore, Maryland 21211
The Johns Hopkins Press Ltd., London

The paper used in this publication meets the minimum requirements of American National Standard for Information Sciences — Permanence of Paper for Printed Library Materials, ANSI Z39.48-1984.

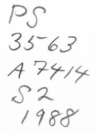

Library of Congress Cataloging-in-Publication Data

Martone, Michael.
Safety patrol: stories / by Michael Martone.
p.   cm. — (Johns Hopkins, poetry and fiction)
Contents: King of safety — Nein — Lost — Parting — The third day of trials — Watch out — An accident — A short, short story complete on these two pages — Carbonation — March of Dimes — X-ray — The safety patrol.
ISBN 0-8018-3602-6 (alk. paper)
I. Title. II. Series.
PS3563.A7414S2   1988
813'.54 — dc19   87-26868
CIP

for Robert M. Sullivan
and for Joseph Geha

All who know me consider me an eminently *safe* man.

Herman Melville
"Bartleby the Scrivener"

CONTENTS

ACKNOWLEDGMENTS

I wish to thank the National Endowment for the Arts and Iowa State University for their assistance during the writing of this book.

I also wish to thank the editors of the following magazines for originally publishing these stories and for permission to reprint them here: *Benzene* for "Carbonation," *Crescent Review* for "King of Safety" and "The Safety Patrol," *Denver Quarterly* for "Lost" and "Parting," *Mississippi Valley Review* for "The Third Day of Trials," *Northwest Review* for "*Nein*" and "An Accident," and *Black Ice* for "Watch Out," which was published as "Lucky One in America." "A Short, Short Story Complete on These Two Pages," "March of Dimes," and "X-ray" were selected by the PEN Syndicated Fiction Project and appeared in the Minneapolis *Star and Tribune* and the Arizona *Republic*.

And thank you Sallie Gouverneur.

Safety Patrol

KING OF SAFETY

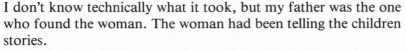

I don't know technically what it took, but my father was the one who found the woman. The woman had been telling the children stories.

She had a telephone number a digit off one that gave a recorded story. Kids would dial, listen, wait through the commercial message. The stories were fables and fairy tales which changed daily, delivered by that voice — I always believed it was a woman from somewhere else trying hard to sound as if she grew up in the Midwest — which spoke all the messages for the phone company. It is the voice that says: We can not complete your call. It is necessary to dial a one. Please try again.

In any case, the real woman gave up trying to explain to her callers that they had reached the wrong number. At first she had thought these were crank calls when all she heard was panting. She called the telephone company. The company gave her the usual song and dance.

She had to be old and alone, a widow, a grandmother with her family out in California.

The kids would call and listen. After dialing the number, they'd exhaust their knowledge of telephone etiquette. They'd tell her to start. They began to cry, hanging on to the phone, startled by this other voice, a voice that sounded frightened and confused, too.

The woman gave up trying to explain, began telling her own stories. She used the library. She bought the big books from remainder tables. She told the callers about her own grandchildren and her children. Family stories. Finally striking up conversations with the callers, she got to know individual children well enough to select something special, perhaps the same special story or a whole series. She started leaving tales unfinished so that the children would call the next day for the conclusion. She's let the children finish the story themselves. "Call back tomorrow."

This went on without parents catching on. They thought it was innocent, darling, their children pressing the oversized receiver to their heads, talking seriously to a recording.

Soon the calls to the real story fell off to nothing. Everyone was calling the woman. Her number became *the* number. My father, who was a switchman at the South Office then, found the woman telling the stories, found her tiny voice.

I was one of those children.

My parents have a picture of me from around that time. I am on the telephone. It is a black-and-white snapshot, but I know the wall phone behind me is yellow. I am in a highchair wearing only a diaper and rubber pants. My skin has that grainy finish. The cord from the phone drops behind me and looks like it runs out of my bare chest up to my arms and fists covering the receiver, my head. I am looking away, my eyes are deep in the cave of my arms. I must have been crying because my eyes are teary. There are flecks the color of the glossy coated stock of the paper in the black irises. They used to print a month and year on the white borders of the square pictures. But that was when the pictures were developed, not when they were taken. A roll of film might stay in a camera for a year. So it is impossible to say when exactly this picture was taken or why or if I was listening to anyone or if I was even talking then. It is one of only a few pictures that is not of a vacation or special event. It's the only record of that wallpaper, cornflowers in baskets, now three or four layers beneath the paint and paneling that's been applied since then. It wasn't that long ago but the telephone, the highchair, the rubber pants, the big safety pins in the diaper look rare, museum-quality, so old.

It is funny to watch people talk on the phone because only a few parts of them are involved. It's like they are off dreaming. They are somewhere else. Their eyes stare into the distance. Their bodies limply dangle from what kind of look like nooses around their necks.

I can hardly recall that woman's voice, but I know the story I liked to hear. It was the one about the man and the steam shovel who must dig a hole before the sun sets or they won't get paid. They dig so fast they forget to leave a way out of the pit. But the building is built right on top of them, trapped in the basement. The happy ending is the steam shovel becomes a furnace and the man the custodian. I asked the woman to read this story. I believe she did, and I followed along at home with my own copy of the book. I could hear through the phone when to turn the pages.

My father came home one day—this was much later—and said the company would be closing up all the windows in the switch rooms. You used to be able to see into the buildings, into the frames and switches, from the street. Now the windows are bricked over or there are steel curtains behind the windows which make them look like the buildings still have windows, like the building was like any other building.

A switch room looked like a library. There were even those tall oak ladders on wheels that slid in tracks. The ladders had signs hanging from the step at eye level. They read, Look up before Moving. In the o's of Look there were black dots, pupils peeled to the top of the bigger circles, eyes looking up. The switches had battleship-gray covers to keep the dust out. The covers looked like bindings, uniformed, shelved like encyclopedias. The shelves went to the ceiling. The frames to the far end of the room.

But there was always the click of the switches as the electricity looked for a way from the caller to the one called. My father could follow a call through the building. He bent his head to listen, distinguishing the sounds. The thump when someone somewhere picked up the phone, the brushes sweeping the switches as they counted the number dialed, the kiss at the end when they swung over to connect. All seven connections snapped free when the call ended and someone hung up. He always knew when something important was happening outside the building. The clicks and stutters grew, boiled, ricocheted all around the big room. Finally he would take the headphone and plug into a call using the two alligator clips. He'd listen hard to the voices and decipher the message. There was a steady rain of calls, the word of mouth. Who had been killed? What war? How many dead?

My father probably broke all kinds of rules by bringing me to the switch room in the first place. But sometimes after hours he'd get called in to troubleshoot, and my mother and I would go along. She would sit at the workbench reading *Playboy* magazines taken from someone's locker. A switch would be dissected on the table before her. Its guts spread out over the newspaper covering the spilled coffee. I collected scraps of wire from the floor. Behind the switches the wires were braided into ropes, the ropes to cables. The bright colors of each wire surfaced and sank like fish in a rolling sea.

My father always found the trouble.

Often there were voices talking over the clicks of the switches. A line had been tapped because there was something wrong. The conversations would be piped through speakers. That's what my father listened to while he worked. He listened to these conversations. No real emergencies. The ordinary traffic of chat. People checking in on each other.

When I call long-distance, when I call home now, sometimes, I'll hear one of those conversations again in the shadow of my own mundane call. I'll be talking about the weather and my father will ask if I want to speak to my mother. But I can hear another conversation in the wires, or in the air now, traveling along with mine. Someone will laugh somewhere, describe a day all differently from the one I will be talking about. It becomes too difficult to go on, I get distracted, pulled into the other conversation. "I'll call back," I say, "and get a better connection."

"Do you hear that?" I say. I listen to the whispering. I think it is the very same conversation I heard those nights long ago when my father walked up and down the aisles of switches, plucking out single wires from the mess of wires and attaching meters that measured the current's flow, the resistance.

The boxes that contained the recordings had windows, so I

could see the tapes wind and unwind. Time and temperature, the weather, the very things the people were talking about on the speakers. I saw the storytelling cartridge, as well, spinning, spinning.

For awhile my mother liked to plant things with philodendrons. We had a potbellied stove with the heart-shaped leaves roiling from the vents and hatches and ports. Chests and dry sinks, wash basins and pitchers. She hollowed out an old wood wall phone, and the leaves coiled with the crank, the mouthpiece, hung from the tilted shelf where the phone book would have been perched. She even planted the shotgun my father had gotten for her during the time he worked at night.

The gun probably never would have fired. But the idea was for her to frighten the intruders in the home, to look like she knew what she was doing. There had been a prowler in the neighborhood for a long time. My father had listened helplessly to the conversations at night, people staying up late thinking they had heard something. Sitting at the workbench in the office, a ruined switch before him, there were whispers around him, rumors, gossip. The clicks knitted up the city. Everyone talked about it and the talk came through the switches late at night, ran on the speakers, echoed in the big room.

But my mother hung the gun on the wall, somehow coaxed the vines down the barrel, and the leaves sprouted at the breech. With the room in half-light the gun looked wrapped in barbed wire.

You couldn't kill the stuff. That's why she grew it. Cuttings were always soaking in jam glasses on the window sill above the sink.

My father's phone calls would wake us all through those nights he worked. There was a princess phone in my parent's bedroom. The dial glowed with a kind of blue light the color of the taxi lights at airports. I woke up to hear my mother groping in the dark, talking to herself or my father. Sometimes, she would stay up all night instead, watching old movies. Those nights my father brought her a Buddy Boy sandwich from Azar's. I found the sacks in the morning when I got up, even found a few sesame seeds from the bun sown in the carpet around their chairs.

I like to call them when I travel. I call from the observation decks of tall buildings. There are always phones there, usually around the corners from the gift shops, away from the elevators. I like to look out and tell them what I am seeing.

When the company sealed up the switch rooms my father took me up to the roofs of the buildings after he troubleshot. At the Main Office we'd even go further up to the top of the microwave tower. The pigeons purred in a frequency lower than the transmitters nested around us. On a clear day we could see the next tower on the horizon in each direction looking back at us.

I call from revolving restaurants. Sometimes, I stay on long enough to go all the way around. Sometimes I don't remember, as the view comes around, that I'd already seen it.

Before I was going to school, the company was sending my father to schools. He called from all of the cities I visit now. This was before all the tall buildings, even before direct dial. That is one thing he went away to learn about, direct dial. He was gone weeks at a time. He brought me Tonka trucks of all sorts — fire trucks, delivery trucks, postal vans. They were all metal. The tires were rubber like tires. It made sense. That story I wanted the woman to read all the time had pictures of just such vehicles done up in a metallic crayon wash. I like construction, building. Even now next to the tall buildings are the deep holes and the bright yellow caterpillars crawling around at the bottom of them. I am one of those men you see looking through the plywood. I excuse their dust. I've rushed through a lonely lunch. I don't know anyone in this town. It is what my father must have done when he went away to school. He killed time until the class started or after it was over for the day, watching cranes being built by other smaller cranes, then the cranes building the building.

Maybe he thought about it on the long train rides back home from one of those schools and cities. Maybe it was clear from what was happening once he returned to work in the offices. He began changing things. He would be transferred from one switch room to another. Main. North. South. Times Corners. Poe-Hogland. He went to each with all that he had learned. Somewhere along the line it must have come to him. What he knew now really meant that very soon his job would not exist anymore. In a way he was wiring what he knew and what he had learned and what he was into those buildings so that the buildings would

6   SAFETY PATROL

pretty much run themselves. And these things would come to pass, would happen long before he was even old enough to retire.

Somewhere about this time I became the King of Safety. I rode a float in two parades. One was on Memorial Day and one was on Armistice Day. It wasn't a float but a trailer pulled by a car. The wheels were hidden beneath skirts of corrugated cardboard painted with black and gray tempera. It was supposed to look like a brick foundation. My father rode in the back seat of the company car. He looked back up at me on the trailer. I was sitting on a porch glider. There was a Queen of Safety, too. She was bigger and older, in the other corner of the glider. A sign swayed above us, suspended from a garden trellis stuffed with red and green crepe paper that looked from a great distance like vines and flowers. Along the route of the parade on Memorial Day everyone listened to transistor radios and to the race. I could hear the tinny engines. Except for that the parade was pretty quiet. The nearest band was up ahead marching toward the Memorial Coliseum. I waved and waved. Everyone pressed their heads against the little boxes at their ears. Parnell, the street where they have the parades, still to this day has elm trees. I saw the reflection of the arching branches sweep down the rear window of the car over my father's face. The whole summer was ahead, filled with watching the city cut down trees. But all the trees survived here, came together above like a cathedral. This is what it must have been like when my parents had been children, when the city, it seemed, was entirely shaded.

My parents had sent in that baby picture, the one of me on the telephone, to a contest the company ran. I imagine the company chose the King and Queen at random out of a whole pile of snapshots, the sons and daughters of employees. The company promoted safety. I understand now that safety was something they could promote. They didn't have to sell the phone service. I think safety had to do with calling a Zenith number before you dug near an underground cable. Safety was like the flags all the soldiers ahead and behind us were carrying. There was nothing wrong with safety.

I had the crown for a long time afterward. I kept it on the globe. It fit, and I just now realize that if I had that globe I would actually know how big my head was then, hold it in my hands. A wife had sewn some sequins onto cut and sculptured carpet backing. It was elaborate and pretty, the crown. I lost it and the globe in a move.

In the summers I caught lightning bugs by slipping an empty peanut butter jar around them as they furiously beat the air. They moved so slowly. The ash at the tail end seemed to heat up like a coal in the breeze. I had punched holes in the lid of the jar through Peter's eyes. I put grass and clover inside. In the morning the insects would always be gone. And my father said that they must have gotten out through the holes. I made the holes smaller and smaller. But still in the morning they were gone. They disappeared.

It was much later, I was gone from home then, when it struck me that my father had lied, that all the time he had been releasing the bugs and resealing the jar. It wasn't long ago that I understood that and called him up and ask him about it. He only said, "I thought you knew."

And it was the same thing with my being King of Safety. It was years after the parades. I understood my father wanted to transfer out of the dying switch rooms, find a job that would not become obsolete. He thought safety was safe. There would always be accidents. There would always be death. His child would be his introduction.

I have never been anything else but the King of Safety. I've never won another raffle or bet or game or contest. I've never been chosen or singled out. It is my one moment in life.

I have the photographs from that day. My feet did not touch the floor of the float but slid back and forth above it as the lawn glider glided. There was a little fountain, too, that had water. The company symbol on the side of the car looks kind of like a cap with ears. My father's face is in the shadow of the roof of the car, but he is looking this way. Did he get the idea about safety during the parade? Or was this just the first step as he untangled himself from the switch rooms? What had he learned by the time we pulled into the lot at the Memorial Coliseum, filled with all the old soldiers in their tight uniforms?

While he worked for Safety I tied his ties. My father sent me five or six at a time. I tied them all at one time, one after another, leaving the skinny end as long as I could so he would be able to slide the tie knotted over his head. The ties are ruined this way. He never learned how to make the Windsor knot or the half-Windsor or even the four-in-hand though I offered to teach him.

In the mirror I kind of looked like him. But I never would have bought those ties. And sometimes my mother would call, frantic because a knot had come undone. I would have to talk her through on the phone. I would look in the mirror going with the mirror's left and right, under and over. I listened to my mother struggle with the tie and the cord of the phone. She'd choke and gasp. She'd sob. I'd hear the gentle slap of the fabric on the mouthpiece. Her hiss, the hiss of the polyester.

I used to call myself person-to-person when I traveled. Really I was calling my parents to let them know I had arrived safely. The operator would say my name, and my father would say "he's not here." I could still do that, call and ask for myself, but I am older and have a credit card. I punch the numbers in after I hear the tone. That voice comes on when I finish, the one the phone company has had for years, and says "thank you."

Besides, I am up in the air when I call, on the observation decks of tall buildings.

Now I want to take three minutes and tell my parents that I can see three states and an ocean from where I am standing. The time on the phone is like the time I get on the binocular machines they have on these observation decks. One second you're looking out into the night trying to make out something. Then that black curtain they have inside snaps down. It's discipline, I say to myself. "I've got to go," I tell my parents after the first three minutes.

Once in Chicago in the black Sears Tower, I watched a formation of helicopters emerge from a park by the lake, rise and orbit the building below where I was standing looking down. "I bet that's the president," my father said. "He's supposed to be in Chicago today. I bet that's him."

I couldn't tell, but one of the helicopters drifted up until it hovered level with my floor. The men in the doorway of the helicopter looked my way steadily. "What's happening?" my mother said. She was on the extension.

By the time the woman died, the phone company had all her

stories on tape. The tapes are still used. My father told me that when she was first confronted with evidence of what she had been doing, she lied. She was afraid, my father said.

When I was older and after my father was working in Safety, I asked him about the switches I had seen in the old offices, the switches marked with a twist of scrap red wire. He told me those had been hot numbers the other switchmen had listened in on. They were people in love with each other and apart. You found them easily because they were connected all night, the magnetism of the current holding the circuit fast. The lovers always thought they were being listened to, my father said, when they were.

"Do you hear something?" one would say every time there was a pause in the conversation. "It's nothing," the other would say. "It's in the phone." My father told me all this though he said he never listened like the other men.

My father was born the day before Christmas, and we always felt bad because he never seemed to get as much as the rest of us. His gifts all came at once. Christmas Eve is the one day he goes out alone. He goes to the 412 Club and Casa D'Angelo and the Hoosier Tap, where friends from work buy him drinks. One of our Christmas traditions is to worry about my father. He makes his way from one bar to the other. He never calls. It is hard to know now if it is real worry or mock worry. He always comes in around the time he was supposed to. The rest of us can eat and open presents. Every year he comes home with a new idea for a drink constructed from different food colorings and fruits. He stands over the blender, crushing ice while we tell him that this is the last year for his running around.

I have a picture of him taken on one of those nights. He is sitting slouched in a kitchen chair, under the yellow wall telephone. There is a different wallpaper on the wall. His eyes are half-closed. His hair is cut strangely. It was the only time he went to that barber. He is holding a bundle of long, thin sticks. My mother gave him switches because he had been bad that year. He looks very pleased and wise. He was feeling no pain, basking in the pop of the flash bulb. He was soaking up the abuse we were giving him, which he has always accepted as our love.

Years later my father will lose his job in the Safety Department during a reorganization. He will spend his last years with the

SAFETY PATROL

company supervising the cutovers in the offices so that they will all have electronic switches, components, solid-state parts. "It is no big deal," he will tell me when I call.

The second parade I was in when I was King of Safety wound through downtown in early November. No one came. It was cold early that fall, and a few years afterward they stopped having that parade. I didn't wave. I huddled beneath an army blanket with the Queen. The little fountain was bone-dry. The metal glider burned in the cold. The parade moved as slowly as it had in the spring. And it was silent. The bands weren't playing because of the chill. Their lips would stick to the brass mouthpieces. The sidewalks were empty. The stores closed. The streetlights came on automatically. Everyone said that it smelled like snow.

I think now I should have been miserable. But for a long time afterward, these were the best moments of my life. My father was in the white car. I saw him watching me as I was being pulled along. The parade shuttled back and forth. It was as if we were looking for a crowd of jubilant cheering people. But, at the same time, we were restrained enough not to break this stately cadence. I felt as if something grand had been visited upon me and every-thing — the buildings and streets of the city — was in order and everything would be preserved and maintained by this cold. We were barely moving, and, though I do not have a picture of this parade, it felt as if we were a picture and capable of telling volumes to the people who would come upon us in the future.

The voice of the woman who tells stories is not the way I remember it. I can hear something disquieting in the voice. I believe it has to do with talking to no one but a machine.

The windows of the telephone building were bricked-in out of fear of terrorist attacks.

The prowler was arrested only two doors from my parents' house while in the act of raping a woman who lived alone.

On the Empire State Building I can go outside, stand on the platform and pretend to see my parents' house, miles away. I like the elaborate precautions, fences and pikes that curl in with sharpened points. I have been to the pit back in Indiana where the stone for the building was cut. All the way down the building would be the limestone fossils arranged in the strata of prehistoric life.

They say that time slows down during accidents, that every-thing becomes very clear. I have never experienced the sensation, having never been that close to death. I look west to Indiana. The wind blows my tie into my face. I try to arrange my hair. The quarry is as deep as the building is tall. I imagine reading the façade while plummeting along the side of the building. I try to imagine my brain working that fast, attempting to arrange the clams and worms into some story.

I've called home. I talked to my father. In the silences between descriptions he pushed buttons on his phone. The tones came together into simple little songs, nursery rhymes, lullabies. It wasn't much and he told me it wasn't hard to do. And time was passing.

I love this, the Empire State Building and its blown crowd of people, observing. We hold back, holding back, each toying with the idea, each of us finding inside some argument against that jump.

NEIN

My grandfather writes to me about what might be the last gasoline price war ever. The price of regular is already 29.9 cents a gallon. At the Lassus Brothers station up Main Street from the Standard where my grandfather works, regular is two cents lower and another penny will come off by the end of the week. He writes about the lines of cars that inch into the station, how happy the drivers are when he leans down to the opening window. The drivers chatter on after asking for the fill-up. They recall the summer of their first car when, even then, gas was more expensive. They hitch their thumbs over their shoulders indicating five or six red tins, the size of dictionaries, in the back seat. "Those too." Some of them ask again if the numbers can possibly be right, and Grandfather bends over and explains the war to the customer. The pump dings in the background, and the bell in the garage dings as other cars pull up. The Lassus Brothers and the Gladieaux Company, the small local concerns, are gambling this last time, this winter. Since the major companies were buying out the owner-operated dealerships, the owners also went along and cut prices. Their days seem numbered anyway. Gulf and Conoco have already pulled out of the city, and Shell is wavering and has begun to offer cutlery again. With the prices this low, no one is using the self-service pumps to save the penny. So Grandfather has a chance to talk to people in the cars. The heat escaping through the windows is the only warmth he can get. The cars keep coming, one after the other. No one bothers to use their credit cards. There is no need to go back inside and run them off. There are many out-of-state plates, Michigan and Ohio. People driving up from Indianapolis are the only ones who seem to be interested in having their oil checked. In Henry's parking lot across the street and the lot by the newspaper building and along the curbs of Main and Broadway, cars idle in harmony. The running lights from other cars as they troll past the double-parked cars define the identical clouds of rising exhaust. The prices will go lower.

Grandfather has worked for Ed Harz's Standard for the last thirty years, part-time after his other job. Although he has retired from City Light, he continues to work for Ed on weekends and nights. When my mother was away at school, he would write to her from the station, sitting on the high metal stool next to the candy machine, using its top for a desk. He would send her money, telling her to use it to buy stamps and write or to have her laundry done there instead of mailing it home. He wrote these messages on the backs of pink customer receipts he found on Ed's desk, or on the reverse of flyers from the Amoco Torch Club. He writes on the other side of the big single-numbered sheet that stands for the day he worked. He has pulled it down from the three-colored Atlas Tire calendar right before he closed up. A quickly scratched note with no subject in the sentences. Some money. An order. A direction. The rest was left to the imagination. Before the price war started, I would get the same type of notes. Now, because he is so busy at the station, he writes them when he gets home or waits until after closing, sending all of his paper tip money or money he has changed into paper. The silver is usually kept for the younger grandchildren. He sends a note about the price of gasoline in Fort Wayne, Indiana. He writes that he is very tired. There is no end in sight.

I think of him at the station. It is one of those old blue and white ceramic tile boxes with glass wrapped around one corner of the front. The oil company wants to change it to the colonial brick façade, cupola and weather vane. Grandfather, on the islands, slides sideways between the pumps and oil cabinets from car to car. "What ja have? What ja have?" Or I can see him angling across the driveway, leaning into the wind. He steps over the driveway hoses that would set off the bells and works his way over to two metal display signs in the one corner of the property. One on springs rocks down and back against the wind. The other, when the wind blows, separates into three sections that swing back and forth, coming together to read in big red numbers "29.9." Grandfather wears a pin-stripe coverall. Over that is a quilted vest, not a new bulky down vest but an actual lining from a coat. On his head is a helmet liner from the Second World War he got surplus. Green wool. On its brim is his union button, a hand squeezing the light out of bundle of lightning. He is carrying a stack of plastic numbers for the sign. It is difficult in this weather to climb the little ladder to reach the sandwich sign on the pylon. It is beneath the twirling orb emblem and the slogan that reads, You Expect More from Standard, and You Get It. As he begins to change the prices, a sudden gust of wind strips the numbers from his arms and carries them down the street. The *ones* vectoring, the *twos* somersaulting to *fives,* the *eights* halving to *threes,* the *zeros* dribbling along the sidewalk. The *nines* of the state sales tax enclose everything my grandfather shouts in quotations of cardinal numbers. He chases them down the street between the celebrating automobiles. The cost is the same. The price is lower still. He writes that no one gets out to help. Everybody honks their horns at once, thinking things have never been so good.

❖

"Think of me," my grandfather writes, "think of me." The letters come to me in bank envelopes, business-size with the plastic window and a silver lining scrolled with insignia so that nothing can be distinguished when they are held up to the light. He is sending money. The letter is folded around the bill and then stapled so, when the letter is unfolded, I must snap the top fold up and the lower flap away from the middle section of the page and the bill extends out from the bottom of the sheet, a tongue. It is always real money, never a check or postal order.

Growing up, the grandchildren are taught never to move anything in Grandfather's house for fear of uncovering another hiding place for his money. He will not use banks except for the envelopes and free desk calendars. Even before the Depression, he refused to invest and still believes a man can weather anything by keeping his money at home. I have found folded bills under lamps and ashtrays, in the phone book. I can make out shadows of coins in the globes of ceiling fixtures, and bills silhouetted in the shades of lamps. I would have to sit in the dark living room, waiting for Grandfather to turn on the one light that would, this week, reveal nothing. All hiding places are that simple. Between the cardboard cover of an album and its plastic wrapping or inside the inner sleeve, a "crispy" would be secreted, forgotten because the record was never played but purchased only for its cover's contribution to some lost filing system. Grandfather has forgotten how much money he made, losing money on purpose in the house, buying only records for himself, and giving the rest away in allowances to his daughter and son and to their children. To me. This is the way around taxes, which he associates with death. He writes that in this way an inheritance will not be taxed but given outright. After he dies, he wants us to sell everything in the house, even the light fixtures. What we find, we can keep as if the money had slipped out of a pocket long ago and lodged between the cushions of the sofa.

My mother writes that when she went away to school her father would write, "Think of me." Now, when she closes her short notes, crowded with weather and unspoken superstitions, Mother writes, "Think of your grandfather," as unthinking, as conventional as "yours truly."

❖

I think of my grandfather at the filling station. He is writing a short note with a black crayon on the back of a calendar leaf. He writes, "Happy Birthday to me." It is his birthday, and the only money I have has come with the announcement. He stands at the

16   SAFETY PATROL

high table inside the station, peeling the silver and black paper spirally from the crayon. The credit-card machine is on the table next to this letter, and he clicks the lever up and down — each place a lever, a scale from 0-9 — changing the numbers and their combination on the stamp as he composes. "The price still falls." On the windows in front of him are the dark sides of display signs, powered by tiny motors and flashlight batteries. The tiny electric whine rotates larger and larger gears until on the other side a Day-Glow disk moves beneath a cutout cover of sunrays and urges, as it radiates, to summerize your car. Next to it, wipers sweep back and forth over a smiling cardboard family. Racing around the dark, closed driveway, the neighborhood kids in their heavy winter coats circle on stingray bikes, running over the hoses, thinking they are ringing the bells. But either they are not heavy enough to set them off or Grandfather has turned the bells off with the lights. The only sound, besides the boring of the displays, is the running of the toilet in the ladies' room around the back. In the tank, Grandfather has hidden a delivery payment for the truckman who will come early the next day, and the balance of the plumbing tips the secret. Ed pays cash.

Ed Harz, who owns the station where Grandfather works, came to America between the wars. He found the railroads now being worked by the Irish, stayed on the Pennsy long enough to make it to Fort Wayne, where he had relatives. He worked in one of the breweries. During the Second World War, he worshipped at one of the secret masses said in German and later those Sundays led a contingent of German citizens out to the prisoner-of-war camp to give the inmates lessons in English. After the war, Ed bought the filling station and hired Grandfather. Many German residents started their own businesses and provided jobs for the prisoners who stayed after the war or came back after returning first to Europe to gather families. Most of the service stations are run by German families. Ed also helped to start the Fort Wayne Sports Club after the influx of new German families. It was organized to support a semipro football team in a country that did not call it football. The club had since become a place to drink Bergoff Beer smuggled in from Chicago and talk, in German, about the price of gasoline. Ed is at the Sports Club as my grandfather writes this letter.

Grandfather writes, "I want you to learn German in school." We are not German. At the station, he has always felt uncomfortable with the other men who could speak two languages. "Talk to a man in his own language." My family knows no other way of speaking.

Reading Grandfather's letter, I can hear Ed again.

Ed's accent now is very faint. An accent I imagine has to do with selling gasoline. The smell of gasoline. Gothic script on his breast pocket. I imagine hearing myself asking Ed for a fill-up in a low low German voice. Something a teacher would repeat as an interesting cultural aside. Phrase-book knowledge:

Bitte volltanken!

"It is all I ask," Grandfathers writes. This is certainly true, I think as I pluck the bill from the day that was his birthday. The staple remains fixed to the letter. I set about learning another language.

❖

I hold the envelope up to the light. The contents are masked; the return is penned out. Grandfather. Long before the price war, his station participated in a sweepstakes, a giveaway of cars and cash. With every purchase, no, maybe none was necessary, the customer received a packet of gummed stamps in sealed envelopes. The picture on the stamp, one of a number of professional football players, had to be matched with an identical picture on a playing card. Various combinations and numbers of players counted for different prizes — three won ten dollars, five won twenty-five, six won fifty, and nine won a new Mustang. The one stamp you needed never appeared. Regular customers all had the same incomplete card in the glove compartment. Grandfather would loiter around the car, polishing the outside mirrors as the customer opened the new envelope. He told them not to be disappointed when they received another Fuzzy Thurston, "Why only last week a man in Huntington won ten dollars," then asked for the stamp to take home to his grandson who collected them, "if you've already got that one." Grandfather brought home cartons of the sealed envelopes and handfuls of ripped-open envelopes from losing patrons. He would go through them for me. "This is a lucky one. I can tell." I would hold each one up to the light trying to save time and avoid opening every one, but all of them were shielded and had to be ripped open anyway. I would only find another Mick Tingleoff or Gale Sayers, never the elusive Lou Groza. Now, I believe I would have been ineligible anyway. Being family. Perhaps Grandfather did not know the rules. It was after that contest that the law was changed in the state, and the company had to publish the probability of winning, with a statement about all prizes being awarded. Giveaways became less common. Many stations began selling children's toys, Corning Ware, Hummel figures. They gave away ice scrapers and ball-point pens. I think now that the winning stamp might never have been minted. Grandfather saved many of the stamps, thinking they would become valuable some day, and sticks them on the backs of the envelopes of his letters, like Christmas seals.

❖

Grandfather writes, "Use this money to make friends." The money talks. "Buy a girl a Coke. In a glass. From a fountain. Not a can." As Grandfather writes, the wind dies in the color pennants, strung out over the dark driveway. The filling stations on the other corners are closing. Their lights go out. Their signs stop revolving. Someone leans over to a pump and takes a last reading, noting it on the clipboard dug into his hip. On a siding behind the newspaper building, boxcars of newsprint in huge rolls are being unloaded. The new construction on the hospital continues through the night. The open elevator the bricklayers use is yellow, festive, a cage of lights. They have rigged a Christmas tree on the top, and it is still there after Christmas, a skeleton with lights, going up and down.

"Who are you writing, Jim?" Betty asks Grandfather. He is sitting at Ed's desk by the phone because Ed will call in a bit. The bottle of Pepsi Grandfather has been drinking from is next to him. There are salted peanuts at the bottom that look like mixing beads in a bottle of dark polish. "You got enough light, Jim?" Betty asks. Betty has no phone in her apartment and uses the station's pay phone. "My grandson," he says. "He is learning German." And he will tell her everything. The candy bars he once took home for me. Powerhouse and PayDay. How I remind him of Efrem Zimbalist, Jr. "I send him a little something every week," he says.

The pay phone rings. She turns to answer it, then disappears behind a curtain of fan belts. Grandfather writes to tell me that another language is not easy to learn, that one way of speaking is enough for most people. I should not give up. "Think of me."

The phone rings on Ed's desk. Grandfather answers it.

"How did we do, Jimmy?" says Ed. He is at the Sports Club. There would be drinking songs. Grandfather tells him of the good day. "We can afford it, what, Jimmy? Prices this low," says Ed softly. Grandfather hears him say something gruff off the phone and laughs as he returns. "The tires, Jimmy, they're in the bay?"

Grandfather walks Betty back to the Poagston Arms, and he waits in the lobby while she runs in to find a stamp for him.

"I will pay you back, Bet," he says. He leaves, walking by the station. The windows of the service bay doors still have the outline of fake snow in the corners from the holiday decorations. Stopping at the mailbox, he slides his tongue across the stamp. His lips dry instantly in the cold wind. He slips the stamped letter onto the tongue of the mailbox slot. Checks that it is gone. Checks again. He reads the pickup schedule and checks his watch, cocking it to the streetlight. He notices how close the clouds are to the bank tower and how they are lined with the pure yellow sodium light of the new downtown. Two days later, the present arrives with his letter, and I go through everything again, every step he takes, two days ago, to get home.

❖

I am learning a new language. I write to my grandfather. He writes back. "What do you want, a Willkie button?" Or I can hear him reverse the accents on the word *Broadway* as he teases about how far I think I am going, where I think I am getting off. He flexes the muscles of his forearm and says to the younger grandchildren, "You want to take a ride?" as they take turns swinging back and forth on the tense arm. He is making up stories about me. I grew up listening to my future. "The FBI.

Solve mysteries. Think about the FBI." In a few days, I will receive a Willkie button. It arrives. A stylized picture of an airplane flying very high and the legend:

Straighten Up and Fly Right.

My mother writes to say she will no longer understand what I am saying. She believes that I will begin running words together in English since this is all she knows about German. At her father's insistence, she sends a German chocolate cake. I share it, as I am told to do, with the woman in the mailroom and with the postal carrier. They ask about my button, and I tell them about Wendell Willkie and the ironic expression of petty awards. My grandfather kept hundreds of facsimile campaign buttons after a promotion ended at the filling station. The company gave these buttons away with flash cards on their history. Petty awards. Grandfather kept as many Willkie buttons as he came across. A bulletin board at his home is covered with Dewey's buttons and Al Smith's and Landon's buttons with his picture surrounded by an aura of the sunflower. Around the edges of the board in the cork lining, Grandfather's union buttons proceed through the years, silver stems, changing colors annually — from orange, yellow to blue or green. If you look closely, you can see the tiny union label of the printing trade that made the button for Grandfather's union. It is there, next to the hand squeezing the bouquet of lightning.

❖

I have learned the language well enough to translate the political slogans on the Willkie buttons. I send Grandfather a composition, in German, mainly in the present tense, referring again and again to incidents in his life. In English, I suggest that he show the above to Ed and let him judge my skills. Next Monday, Ed comes to my grandfather's house to pick up his carton of eggs. My grandfather buys a number of eggs wholesale for his friends and sells them at cost. They sit in the kitchen. Ed assembles his dozen, checking his eggs by holding them up to the light and places them in an old gray pressed-paper carton, turning the eggs the same way. Grandfather shows him this letter. Ed scans the letter quickly, stopping on a word now and then.

Looking up at Grandfather, he says shyly, "Jimmy, is this true?" And Grandfather will ask what it is he has read. And Ed will only say, "All true, Jimmy, all true?" A letter will be written that night.

❖

I receive a letter that must be from Grandfather. I recognize his hand on the envelope. I cannot see through to the letter, but I can make out the darker rectangle inside. An old football stamp seals the smile of the fold on the back. Because I have learned German, perhaps there will be two bills. More friends. Instead, I find when I open the envelope, not the usual folded scrap of paper with money but another envelope. And that is all.

The envelope is a smaller stationary size, sealed also and addressed to Grandfather, addressed with the appellation "Herr," in another hand, in real pen and ink. The envelope is an off-color, but it might once have been white. The stamp is foreign and canceled by the United States Army sometime in 1946. The return is a street in Vienna. I do not want to open it, something that has been written and sealed that long ago. I picture Grandfather slipping the envelope inside the other one and then addressing it to me. Where had he hidden it in his house? With the money? With the coffee cans of silver in the cold, summer furnace? Why had I not seen this before, an old letter, among the other things he collected — big-band albums, tire gauges, reproductions of American documents? I leave the letter unopened. The next day and the next and every day after that for several weeks, more of the same envelopes arrive in the same manner. Each with another envelope inside. They look slightly counterfeit, with the extra line for the country like a symbol more detailed than the thing it stands for. I keep the letters in a pile, careful to retain the order in which they came to me.

My mother writes, "Well, what is the story? Why aren't you writing to your grandfather?" I do not know why I am not writing to Grandfather. I suggest it is the high cost of stamps. I do not have time with my studies and all. I have nothing to say. I know I am supposed to translate those letters, and for some reason, maybe even privacy, I do not want to be involved in their meaning, in understanding them for someone else.

One weekend Grandfather calls. He is calling from the station. In the background I can hear the persistent ding of driveway bells and the exhalation of the hydraulic lift. Periodically, comes the rapid fire of pneumatic drills, backing off lug nuts after tightening them, and barely comprehensible German above the racket, which becomes a shout when the noises cease.

"What, Grandfather?"

I can see cigarettes burning evenly in ashtrays by the cash register, where they have been left when the attendants went out to the pumps. Grandfather calls me a pet name, coaxing me to translate the letters. He explains how they came to him. "I heard General Mark Clark on the radio after the war and I did what he said to do." Ed's voice breaks in over the noise, the soft *w* becoming a pointed *v*. "Jimmy, Jimmy, we need you."

"Do what you can for me," Grandfather asks. That night I begin to translate the letters.

❖

They are from a man named W. Gabauer of Vienna. The first letter, "I thank you, and my family thanks you for this paper and pen with nibs (I am not sure of this) so that I can write to you for all your gifts. This paper, this is the sheet." Grandfather seems to have found out about the Gabauers through a reconstruction scheme of the Third Army. The family is similar to his own — a young boy who has known nothing but the war and an older girl, Frieda, who "is learning English now, Mr. Payne, so that she can work in the American Army Bank."

"We have been cleared of everything now," he writes. "It is terrible to have a past." This in capitals. There is a long section recalling the inflation between the wars. "It must not happen again, Mr. Payne. Your army lets us work and controls the price of things. But we survive because of you."

Grandfather has sent them nonperishable food, paper, thread and needles, candles, perhaps some clothing, buttons, tin foil. "Your family is giving all of this up for us." Then long sections on the nature of victor and vanquished and victim. Frieda continues to learn English. He writes at length of peanut butter. They have never seen it before and are unsure what to do with it. There is a letter describing the ruins of a city, a bombed-out building, lines of people moving rubble from one pile to the next, waiting for food, for medicine. "You must not feel sorry for us, Mr. Payne. With your help, we will be just like new." This last phrase supplied, in English, by Frieda.

The packages keep arriving — picture magazines, chocolate, Spam, Quaker Oats, pencils, metal toys. Everything is duly noted, and gratitude is shown for each. The pronouns change to familiar. "The whole neighborhood came together today," he writes, "and everyone brought their American peanut butter. We eat it every way. It is so good." Ribbons, combs, rubber bands, zippers, erasers, popcorn. "What is popcorn?"

I realize that Frieda knows more and more English. She will receive the position at the bank, because she is good with numbers. She writes short notes in English which her father includes with his letters. She writes that she understands Americans better now that she understands what they say to one another. It is a funny language, full of things that mean many things.

Mr. Grabauer describes the spring in the mountains, a day in the life of the family, homesick soldiers. He is grateful for the tobacco and the pipe Grandfather has sent.

"I cannot make you understand," he writes. "You must stop sending so much. The whole family works. I do not mean to offend."

More letters arrive and Grandfather leaves them unopened, as I did, stacks them neatly, imagines what they might say, and goes to assemble another box. He crumples newspaper for packing, the classified so that there will be no mention of the war. Perhaps, Mr. Grabauer will read the want ads and come to America with his family. He could work for Ed. Grandfather would give him his job. Grandfather lines an old cardboard Eckrich meat box with gray paper. He thinks about what a family would need and would not ask for. He thinks of paper clips and toothpicks, towels and soap, string and marbles for the boy. Do they play marbles? He will ask Ed indirectly. Hash, another can opener, dried milk, flour. Today, he will drive to the post office, the first time in years. He picks at the ration stamp in the corner of the windshield. There is plenty for everyone. Things haven't been this good in years.

❖

"Why didn't you let Ed translate the letters?" I ask him.

"It was family business," he says as I spread the letters out on the kitchen table and arrange them by date.

"See, Grandfather, the little line through the *seven* so they won't confuse it with a *one*. They do that with a *Z* too. Look." I trace through the letters, stopping, now and then, to mention peanut butter or Frieda's progress toward her goal. I thank him for everything.

"No. No more," I am translating. I ask him why he didn't even open the letters.

"It was history," he says. "I saved it for you."

I translate the last few letters right there in front of him. It is the first time either of us has read them. "Write to us," it says, and I see the family in Europe one last time, still waiting for a word they could now translate. The whole correspondence running out becomes dear as I let Grandfather read along in Frieda's uncertain idiom to the point where I with my languages, where the family with its letters, where no one needs anything any more.

LOST

Mice had gotten into the basement where he slept. Someone had left the garage door open. He heard them in the dark, running over the indoor carpeting. Hugging the walls, he imagined. Once he was awake he couldn't go back to sleep. It wasn't the mice. He knew the mice wouldn't bother him. There was the sound of claws in the rug, the chatter on the linoleum by the door. He heard them working through the old toys, records, moving things on the floor, touching them. Shoes. His clothes.

He stood up and thought for a second, placing the Ping-Pong table, the air-hockey set up, the pinball. Things on legs.

Near the door he felt for the freezer, white and cold. He stood and waited for the compressor to start up. When it did he opened the chest and the light came on. It was filled with white, stone-shaped packages of the family's meat. Each was stamped with MAPLETON SLAUGHTER and NOT FOR PROCESSING. Their own steers.

He was naked and cold. He left the lid up and got his clothes from across the room. He dressed with the light from the freezer, the air above it white and swirling down over the sides. He closed all the doors and went upstairs, where he sat at the kitchen table until it was light enough to see the cornfield down in the bottom.

This was the second day they would look for the boy in that corn-field.

He had called his girlfriend back East to tell her what he was doing on the farm near Turin, Iowa, again. She had been mad because he reversed the charges and forgot about the hour. The farmer had a daughter. Besides, no cornfield was that big, she said, and he tried to tell her about it. Then he said there was pop-corn in the next field, and the man who owned it told him he could keep what he gleaned in the fall if he came back to help at harvest. He told her about the noise they made and the noise the helicopters made. The faint smell of chemicals.

"You should see it," he told her. He was in the back bedroom, sitting on the platform bed. Airline posters were on the walls. "They'll bring in some psychic soon. The dogs tomorrow." The psychics come after the dogs. He tried to figure how he could figure the odds on such a thing.

That morning there were lights in the field. He could see them out beyond the channeled Little Sioux River. A tractor with an implement was on the road, and the sunlight caught on the peaked irrigator. The boy's family lived in a rented house left standing at a section corner for some sentimental reasons. Some-one's first home. There were many children. Everyone who was searching told him that this one always called you by both your names.

When the family he was staying with talked on the telephone, they used short sentences, a few words, as if someone were listen-ing, as if at any moment the line would have to be cleared for some emergency. He had listened as the farmer walked back and forth with the portable phone, its antenna scraping the walls each time he turned. The farmer had said, "Yes, yes, yes," calmly.

The farmer explained it to him once. He said it was a habit of party-line days. People listened in because they had nothing bet-ter to do. Everyone knew the line was in use because the number of rings determined who the call was for and everyone's phone rang.

"It's how I learned to count," the farmer had told him. "The longer you talked, the lower the voltage would go and the more the phones got picked up." The voice you were talking to got fur-ther and further away.

"Do you want to come with?" the farmer was saying to him now. Already he could see out on the bottom and the cornfield where the boy was.

The field was known as Cottonwood for the trees that had been there, and the field ran right into the fields on all sides of it. There was no fencing anymore. The animals were pastured in the hills bordering the bottom or confined in new buildings near the old barns. The big machinery could wheel around without hitting anything.

Cars and trucks were nosing over into the ditches on either side of the road to Onawa. A crowd was gathering near a car with flashing lights. He saw all this from a great distance, so he really didn't see it at all, just imagined he saw it from the day before. The men were sitting on tailgates; the women were pouring coffee.

The farmer asked him again, and he said that he would go along. He found himself, his body and legs, stretched out in a lounge chair, covered with sections of newspapers, parts he'd read to keep awake and then spread out over himself to stay warm in the dark house.

He heard the microwave talking to the farmer, who was heating up water for coffee, the chimes and tunes of the calculator he was using to figure stops or calls or puts or something. The farmer was moving grain from last year. He sold a little bit over a long time, hedging the market. The boy was lost in this year's crop. The field was still green. The leaves on the plants still curled from the night but opening. The ears were filling out and heavy. The field they called Cottonwood was the one he helped plow in the fall. The farmer was punching a number on the wall phone in the kitchen.

He had come to Des Moines to work as an actuary for one of the insurance companies. The building where he worked was the only landmark in the city. It had a three-story, red neon umbrella on the roof. The sign looked best in the rain, at night in the rain. His girlfriend worked for one of the Big Eight firms, the one that did the Oscars. She was studying for her first actuary exam and had supervised audits in Erie and at Quaker Oats in Cedar Rapids. When she worked in Cedar Rapids, he drove up to see her, taking the only diagonal road in the state.

SAFETY PATROL

"It's so green," she said.

"What do you mean?" he asked her. "No greener than anything else."

"The green is different. It's not a tree green."

She had sent him a copy of the annual report filled with pictures of cylindrical grain elevators, train hoppers, tubs of oats.

He worked with the farmer's daughter at the insurance company and drove her out to Turin when he had nothing better to do. In a way he believed his car needed the exercise.

Around Turin and around the farm were the loess hills, bluffs made up of windblown soil. They were rounded and green, suddenly there between the flat river bottoms. The Maple. The Soldier. The Little Sioux.

"There are hills like this in only one other place on earth, in China, and when I was little I thought that's where the dirt came from, from China. Blown all the way from China."

And the wind was the first thing he noticed once he was out of the car. It came across the bottom from Nebraska.

"That's Nebraska. That line of hills." Another time he watched a storm come from the west, watched the lightning strikes for hours walking toward him.

He walked through a bean field with her, hoeing weeds. They used a length of PVC tubing, rigged at one end with a rope wick kept saturated with the chemical inside the pipe. She still called it hoeing although all they did was touch the weeds with the wicks, careful not to touch the young bean plants. The field was full of volunteer corn, bushy because it grew from cobs lost from last year's harvest. They walked for hours. They kept the hills behind them, into the wind. They touched everything that wasn't a soybean plant, leaving behind a dewy patch on the leaves. She said it wasn't very satisfying. "When you leave the field, everything is still green and not clean, like you haven't done anything," she said. But later when he went back, he looked out into the same field only to see the brown, dying stalks of corn here and there in the neat rows of beans.

He walked through the cornfield, looking for signs of the boy. The rows were clean, cultivated early and shaded now by the crop canopy of the tall plants. He heard the men in the rows on either side of him, walking with him. They talked to one another at the same volume as the rustle produced by their brushing against the leaves. It was hard making out what was being said unless he concentrated, but then he was afraid he would miss something on the ground or on the stalks before him. The tufts of silk on the ears caught him in the same place on his leg as he went along. The tassels above him were extending like aerials, the horizontal arms intersecting each other and spreading a yellow net over the whole green field. He expected to find the boy curled up and quiet on the ground like some animal. And he did startle things. Rabbits and birds flushed and shot away at his feet.

Then they came out of the rows into a bald spot in the field where a pond had been during the planting. It might have been an acre or two and the ground still dark and soft at its lowest point and the grass coming back on the rest. The stunted corn on the edge was yellow from too much water.

He stood there with the men who had been walking on either side of him. They stopped and smoked and talked about crops and animals and the weather, ignoring him. Others moved through the corn around them. He watched the corn move as the people moved through it. In the clearing, they began to tell the stories of the other local tragedies in order to avoid mentioning the boy or the search they were part of now.

They started with fires. The last bar in Turin had been burned down by its owner, and the town was a post office away from being a town. There had been a fire at a confinement operation, and they told of the pile of burned hogs. The fires set in the bluffs. The boys drowned in a grain bin full of soybeans. They held their hands up, counting the fingers they were missing. A farmer's hand had come off clean in a binder. He didn't go into shock but walked home to wait for the helicopter. He left his son to find the hand and put in in their lunch cooler with the block of chemical ice.

"Oh, he was alive all right," someone said about another farmer. "It was a massive shock. His second." They found him the next morning. The lights were on on the combine and him all pressed up against the glass of the cab, looking at the auger still turning on the table below him. He told her on the phone that night, "He was conscious but couldn't move. He sat there. The machine still shaking."

SAFETY PATROL

And now the others looked at him then looked around, ready to head back into the tall corn. He didn't have anything to say though he knew about accidents. There is a list that puts a price on a foot or a whole leg, an arm, a spine. He stood there smiling. He knew his smile would seem to be caused by the bright sun. He told them who he had been staying with. They probably knew already, and they knew what he did in Des Moines, too, probably. They thanked him for coming and helping. But they wouldn't ask anything directly. They would find out in other ways if they wanted to.

He called her that night from a booth left standing near the ruins of the bar in Turin. The elevator was blowing grain from one bin to another. Bugs were sticking to the light above him in the booth. He had walked from the house so as not to bother anyone. He left the farmer reading papers, the daughter sorting her laundry. The end rows of the field edged up to the road.

The first time he called she wasn't there. He talked to the operator before he let her go, asking her where she was and what time it was.

Turin was named after the city in Italy, the daughter had told him. Someone got off a train once and said the hills were the same as those Italian hills. Starting from the post office and his phone booth, the town worked up the seams of three hills. The lights were scattered around and above to the red strobe lights of a translator tower on the crest of the highest hill.

He was always a little sick with the stars, and he looked until he found a plane blinking from east to west and another going in the opposite way. And he wished the phone would ring.

She was in the bar near her house having dinner after work, or she stopped at the convenience store and got caught up watching the neighborhood boys play the one video game the store kept in a closet near the refrigerator motors.

There had been talk while they stood in the clearing that the boy wasn't in the field at all, that maybe the dump should be checked again, the old refrigerators and car trunks.

They had not found the boy again today. The family was beginning to receive all kinds of mail, photos and prayers. A bank account would be opened in the morning.

The soil in the field was the type that caked when it was wet, and their feet were heavy with mud, making it harder to go back into the corn to look some more.

Gumbo. The farmer had told him the name of the soil type was gumbo.

But they went back into the corn and walked the rest of the way through to the end rows. On the edge of the field were the empty fifty-gallon drums that had held the herbicides, only beginning to rust, and on the few remaining fence posts someone had speared the empty seed sacks with their black variety numbers and the cobs with wings.

The next field was fallow, set aside for some federal program, and they were grading and laying tile. He could see a long way. The ditching equipment, a Ferris wheel of buckets, was parked on a slight rise. The field was taken with grasses. Planted here and there in the green were these knee-high wires topped with Day-Glow plastic flags — blue for the buried phone cable, yellow for a gas main, orange for sewage or water or more tile. Since he was near ground level, he couldn't connect the snapping flags into lines. They looked scattered and bunched like flowers. He stood there while others cleaned the mud from their shoes with sticks.

That night by the phone booth, he heard all different types of engines in the bluffs. A tractor in road gear, an insect fogger. Listening, he heard the wind again in the big cornfields nearby. It was like the rustling of paper. Cars of kids passed him heading to the Onawa loop. He would call her tomorrow night from a booth in Onawa near the largest main street in the world. It was really four regular streets running parallel. He will have just finished eating the largest piece of meat he has ever eaten. The farmer will tell him that all the best steaks go to New York.

"Where have you been?" he said to her when he got through.

She told him where she had been.

He told her about the day, the field again, the man trapped and dying in the combine. He told her about Turin, the phone-booth lights, the lights of the town, the stars.

She said she missed him, that she was thinking about him.

He asked her to tell him what she was wearing, what the cat was doing now, the noise he heard. It was a bus going by on the street. And what did she have on and which way was her hair, which barrette. She said she was embarrassed and that this was costing money. And he described where he was out in the open, in the street, the cornfields on both sides. He asked her what she was doing, where she was in the room, sitting down or what, and what she was thinking of. And she said she was no good at this. Then they both said *what*. So he asked her again to tell him how she was sitting, where in the room so he could see her there, so he could imagine her. And then he asked her to touch herself, and she said she was, and he listened for her breathing and then asked her to talk about her body. She said she couldn't. So he just listened as best he could, concentrating on what he heard in the phone, the shell sound at his ear. He thought that he could see her, her eyes closed, the handpiece of the phone held by her shoulder against the side of her head.

Where he slept had no windows, and the door was closed against the mice. The basement was completely dark. It could be night or day, he couldn't tell. The basement had been a playroom for the kids when they were still home. Around him in the dark were stacks of board games and records and bigger games usually only found in arcades. The children had been miles from other kids their age, had played with everything here in the farmhouse basement.

He could feel the bulk of the stuff around the bed, but he couldn't see the outlines of things. So when he was unable to sleep, he felt his eyes opening in the dark, wider than they had ever been, but he still couldn't see a thing.

He thought about the boy still lost after two days of looking and what the psychics would say after seeing with their eyes closed — where he was buried, where he had been washed to. But maybe he was still in the cornfield being missed by the searches as the line swept through this section or that. He was out under the sky, under those stars, under the stand of corn as thick as a lawn.

In the dark basement, he thought of plowing the field last fall. He went back and forth again. The field seemed so much smaller from inside the heated cab. Riding up high, he could see the elevators in every direction. It took him hours to make three or four passes with the five-bottom plow.

The farmer had shown him the controls, how to call up the

numbers for RPMs and exhaust temperature and speed. He touched buttons. The numbers pulsed and rearranged. He lifted and lowered the plow. The tractor folded in the middle when he turned the wheel. There was the pitching in the hydraulics. "Listen, if you miss it, just keep going into the next field." The throttle had a picture of a rabbit and a turtle. Simple. The tractor was red. He kept the wheels on the landside and in the last furrow, dropped the plow, went for miles through the bean stubble. The plow turned over ribbons of gumbo. On the radio the Sioux City public station asked for money. When he looked back he saw a cloud of seagulls above the wake of the plow, swooping down to peck at what he was turning over. More were arriving all the time, white, out of the gray sky. It was something he never expected. He looked toward the house, where he knew they kept binoculars near the window, and he could see that the sun was shining there and on the hills behind the house. And maybe he was being watched.

He wished now that the daughter would open the basement door and find her way to him through the toys. A joke, a joke he thought, but he listened for the strum on the metal stair. He imagined waking up, the daughter becoming solid in the dark, her weight on him before he knows it.

Instead he goes out so he can see again, climbs the high bluff behind the house. At the top the family has a television dish aimed up at the clear night sky.

The loess will not erode if it is cut through at a ninety-degree angle to the grade. Anything less than that and it washes away with the first rain. He can see the sharp lines and the faces of the road cuts and the road itself cutting around the base of the hill.

The television dish is like his company's logo. It is pulling things down from the air. An umbrella upended left to dry on a porch. Nearby is a pile of bones and a rack of sun-bleached antlers probably hauled there by the family dog. There are other things around too — weathered balls and a tumbled fort, a path for steers and dirt bikes. Across the bottom, he sees Nebraska. That's Nebraska.

He goes from one field to the other. His eyes go back and forth over the fields below him. That is what is always done in this country, the going back and forth. It is like reading, not like figuring. The sky is very big, and there are the few lights that farmers leave on all night long. They wouldn't find the boy. He doesn't know how he knows. But he knows.

PARTING

I stutter. Badly. I always have. Through therapy, I learned that it all has to do with the way I've acquired language.

It is hard to explain but it has to do with seeing. My eyes really do roll up inside my head and I'm looking for the right word or syllable or letter. I acquired language in a mechanical age before the pulsing electronic models of the brain. I'm made up of switches, gears, brushes, contacts, solenoid springs, screws. I search by opening drawers, riffling files, sorting through the trash, the business office of metals, green and gray. My machines are the old machines.

I think it has to do with handedness, this stutter.

My father wanted a left-hander perhaps more than he wanted a son. He was always throwing things at me — balls of socks turned inside out, golf balls, Whiffle balls, Ping-Pong balls, balls of string. They came at my face, my head, and my father would project his face, his head along the path of flight. He noted which hand I moved first, which finger of which hand.

Now that I think of it, catching and throwing are the same to me. I have a facility for both in both hands. I make no distinction.

But this is a theory of mine, a hunch. The therapists didn't say one way or the other. They were treating the outward manifestation of how I acquired the language.

My father thought the movement of the left-handed more pure. Especially expressed in the asymmetry of baseball, left-handed was beautiful. I don't blame him. I don't blame him.

Writing this I am like those singers who stutter when they don't sing, whose stutter vanishes when the music begins. One word after another, like clockwork. I can stop my hand, either hand, before the long chorus line of *h*'s steps along this blue rule. What can I say?

There is that motto that circulates through the offices of the world, taped to typewriters and phones, photocopy of photocopy, with the other artifacts of the cute. The you-want-it-when keepers, comics that turn yellow, old postcards from bosses long gone. It says, Be Sure Mind Is Engaged before Putting Tongue into Gear. Exactly. A type of poetry. Rebuild the drive train around the tongue, I say — the shaft of spine, the wires. Into the hand, the hands.

❖

Martin, my friend, and I were in Indiana, Pennsylvania, once, looking around. We had stopped there on our way to somewhere else because we were from Indiana, the state, and we were aimless enough to stop, or maybe that was the whole aim of the trip. Did we imagine a Liberia, a colony of Hoosiers, a diaspora, families keeping alive the old ways, the slow ritual of team basketball? Nevertheless, we stopped and walked around the college they have there, saying we were from the other Indiana. There were few students, gone on the same holiday we were. But when we'd see a cop or a secretary in an office, we'd say we were from the other Indiana and they would always say the same thing: We get your mail.

"That's why we're here," Martin said, "for the mail."

We ended up talking to an African student, surprised that his classrooms were empty. We found him reading the bulletin boards for explanations. We told him, "We're from the other Indiana." It was clever, we thought. And he looked at us earnestly.

"Yes," he said, "my country is always sending its students to the wrong Indiana. It happens often. It's the case." He spoke English haltingly but well, searching for the words. I always marvel at anyone who knows more than one language. I could see he was the type that waited until everything was right, the grammar, agreement, before he spoke.

"We are sent away to one strange place. All we have is a name. And there are many known by that name. There is a California. A California, Pennsylvania."

I remember imagining a ship pulling away from the docks, flags popping. Everyone waves and waves. The sun sets in the wrong place. There's the dusty train station, the borrowed clothes and bag. Somewhere over there is Indiana. The end of the line.

"Why is that?" he asked. "Why is it that several places have the same name? That is not the case where I come from." His face was wide and his eyes. He wanted to know.

And Martin said without thinking, "America is so big we've run out of names."

We've run out of names. Martin.

❖

Once, I took trips all the time with Martin, who never finished my sentences, who never knew where we were going. He waited until I was through talking and had thrown myself back in the seat. My eyes were closed and I was going through what I'd said, rubbing that place behind my ear. "What you mean to say," he would say, and tell me. And then, "Where are we?" and I'd look out, the navigator, and things would be flying by, disconnected signs, markers, arrows, signs that referred to other signs.

Martin calls the Indiana toll road the Bermuda Triangle of highway travel. It is disorienting. The cornfield, a visible magnetic field, changes intensity and color with the layout of the crop rows. The lines of cars and trucks spaced and stretched for miles. They don't move, because we're all moving at the same speed. The pull of the ditch, the siren. The main street of mid-America, the rest stops named after poets and coaches. It's a long sleep. Radios jam from all the iron dust. Time doesn't change. There are sudden sandstorms. Fog like mold on bread. Suddenly we are in Ohio, Chicago. The truck we'd been following — it bristled with antennas, its lights flicked each time it passed us — has disappeared.

This last trip I took with Martin, is it the last trip I'll take with him? I've always wondered. Will this one be? This one? The time we came back from New York — for a long time that was the last trip.

I've said good-bye to all of it, to going.

The truth is I can hardly accelerate up to the speeds necessary. I've found that I am repeating what I have just said. I haven't done that since I was a kid and the therapists suggested it as a way to make me conscious of what I was saying. Word for word, under my breath, an echo. After a while I didn't think about it. I want a glass of water. I want a glass of water. The second sentence was easier, slowed down, sorted out. I saw the hooks and eyes. It wasn't an echo. It was more like going over a signature slowly, staying in the lines. I can't possibly keep up anymore. I find I am often left speechless. The subjects are tattered paper under the wheel. The strange mailbox that is made out of the old plow, the pump, is behind me before I can even begin to begin to speak. It is not an echo. The sentences are not coming back. They bounce off the world. The radar of my own language closes in on me. There is a deer. A pig. A cloud. A tree. A car. These things are coming on too fast. These things are already gone too soon. No planned trajectory. No way to plot their courses.

I'm afraid, Martin. I'm afraid.

Long trips by car were the only times we had to talk. Phone calls, impossible. The stammer on long distance, the tick of a meter. That's it, isn't it? To be in a car is to be in a moving parlor, to leave an exhaust of words.

But this last trip could be the last trip. Because it is getting harder for me to speak, and the distance between us now, the space we shuttle back and forth in, is not great enough. What? I might utter a paragraph in an hour. And patient Martin could drive a Mack truck through the silences.

❖

PARTING   39

Martin likes to say that the job he does now for the Labor Department is the exact same thing Kafka did for Czechoslovakia. I don't know if that's true, but he says it often.

Martin works in the District in the government's own workers' compensation, an investigator. He is a GS-12 now, I think. His office is in one of those buildings downtown that can go no higher than thirteen floors because nothing in the city can be higher than Liberty or Freedom on the Capitol dome. That's why it's such a sad town, Martin says. It all ends at the thirteenth floor. Unlucky — no way around it.

In that building he reads files of claims government workers make, claims of injuries suffered on the job, in the line of duty, above and beyond the call. There are the things you'd expect, the usual accidents of the motor pool, the falls from buildings, office chairs that crumple, the chemical spills, the fires in warehouses. In this way the government simulates our world, its acts of God. But Martin must read about other accidents unique to the bureaucracy so large, the daily toll of service. The pale-green computer screen, the pastel shades of copies, the shades of language, the color of walls in offices that hum, the white lights and shirts, the colors of skin. What he hates is that he gets paid not to believe people who have headaches, undiagnosed lower-back pains. He must start from the position that the mumbling, the hand-washing have nothing to do with the job, that it's all unconnected or even faked.

Poor Martin — to work up ways not to believe, the advocate who punches holes in the cases for saints.

Maybe it's easy. I don't know.

It hasn't soured him on the species. His suspicion is professional. He leaves it on the thirteenth floor. But he carries around these stories. When he thinks of seeing, he is reminded of the blind man. When he hears, he knows he is hearing. And his limbs bud and grow all the other limbs that have been lost.

As we drive, he drives through my silences, between my words. The light is low from the instruments, just touches his cheek. The window behind him is black. Half his face is how I think about him now, his profile, round chin, the nose and mouth. That mathematical symbol, more than and equal to. And in the window, the other side of the face, milky. Skin. I remember remembering smearing white Elmer's Glue on my hand, letting it dry and peeling off long whole strips of fingers, the creases and prints, the topography and whorls of knuckles and nails. The other side of Martin's face in the cold window kept its eye on the road.

The road was in Ohio, wide Ohio. Or Pennsylvania wider still. And Martin was telling amputation stories.

Amputation stories are like ghost stories. There is nothing to them beyond the telling of them. The ghosts make you draw closer around the campfire. Amputation stories, too, make you want to wrap your arms around yourself.

How much of me goes before I'm gone?

Really the stories are about machines. Our marriage to them. Limbs are given *to* the machines, that comes up, to the machine, a type of marriage. Machines amplify our own body's levers — the legs, the arms, the fingers. These become ghosts, lost. Machines amplify the body, make it louder.

I remember remembering the time I sat on the copier in the office and the stripped-down picture of my butt emerging, what? like something being born or passed. The new workplace is all about light and language. I remember the cold glass and the green light rolling below me, my feet not touching the ground. I gave the copy to the woman I was with. Then she rested her white breasts on the glass. She liked me, she said, because I didn't say much, and turned away to look back over her shoulder at me and laugh as the light played over her and the fan came on and rumbled the machine and the little closet where we were. It's all high contrast, her nipples black and scratchy with toner, the depth all washed out, overexposed. The mole still floating there, too, with the dust and motes of the glass. It's on good bond. There was static in the room. Our life slipped into two dimension, plane geometry, depth removed. But real amputations are still a matter of the solid and what Martin was saying sat there, something with a life of its own.

❖

There was this man who lost all of his fingers to a machine. I think a machine that trimmed paper. It had a harness for safety that was supposed to clear the hands each time the blades descended. The device had been adjusted by the man working the machine the shift before. When the new man started this work he didn't check the play, and on the machine's first cycle, trusting it to pull his hands clear, the blades came down and all his fingers were off at once.

"Now the interesting part," Martin was saying. When the machine opened up again he could see his fingers where they had fallen perfectly as if they had been placed there, fanned out the precise distance apart from one another. "He then reached inside, he told me this," Martin said, "he reached inside to pick up his fingers. He forgot that he didn't have anything left to pick up his fingers with. And the machine was still going. But this time when the blades closed down his hands were pulled clear by the safety device."

It was Ohio. And it must have taken me a county at least to exclaim. "Really," and then under my breath again, really, a township at least. Really.

"Really," Martin said.

I remember thinking about the engine of the car, a Dodge, the old slant six. I thought how all those different operations were happening at once. The pistons all at different points in the cycle, the cam shafts timing and the rockers lifting, the valves, the flywheel flying, the distributor distributing. And if you froze it at one instant, the whole show was being run on only one cylinder and inertia, the tendency to remain at rest or to stay in motion.

It was night in Ohio. And the radio was talking, too. The talk shows of the clear-channel stations. I had a bet with a friend that there were more songs written about telephones than cars. I thought if you thought about it there would be hundreds of songs about wrong numbers and long-distance operators and information and late-night calls and arranging rendezvous and calls to repairmen to fix the phone, no answers, busy, dead lines, crossed wires. The song is just voice. And on the phone a disembodied voice at your ear, the privacy of the private line, the party on the party line. Besides, Bell was a therapist. To him the phone was a device that facilitated the acquisition of language. The instrument is a sentimental favorite, far more terrifying to the deaf and dumb than a speeding automobile.

That songs should be written about cars seemed like the conclusion everyone would jump to. It was a sucker bet.

Especially those songs about crashes, wrecks, accidents, death. Or traveling like I did with Martin, cruising on the road, a fabled love of motion and moving. You put poles and wires and miles between where you are and where you're going.

Now here at night in Ohio in a car with Martin there was a kind of nexus — the radio, the callers, the music, the road, the wires, the waves, all of these connections. The voices talking on the show of talk were making a music, a song about singing. What was said meant nothing. Talk for the hell of it. Talk just to hear oneself talk.

"The new section of the drill pipe came down from the derrick too fast," Martin was saying. "This new kid had his foot over the hole, and when the pipe came down and sumped into the hole the kid started yelling, 'Get it off my foot! Get it off my foot!' and the diesel idled down. The local said, 'Step back, son. You ain't got no foot.'"

This is indeed like stories around the campfire. I remember the story of the lovers in a car telling stories, ghost stories, being afraid, wanting to hold each other, creating stories that gave them excuses to do so. And they are telling a story about a man with hooks, a murderer, a nut. The woods, the night. There is scratching at the door of the car. The lovers tease each other. Their imagination. Then they believe and tear out of there in the car. They travel miles with the hook hooked on the door handle. It dangles there. They discover it when they are safely home.

I was always quiet around campfires. To stutter is to sound afraid. No rounds for me, no verses. The night on those nights was vast. The sparks flew up. If I spoke I sounded as if I were afraid. I was afraid to speak.

Outside now I know are strip mines. There are crossed picks on the maps. I wish I could see the shovels, the pulleys and cables, the draglines, the little houses where the operator sits, runs the machine as big as an office building. The little crossed picks don't begin to represent what is going on outside our windows as we race along.

The lovers, the car, the man, are folklore. I have heard about them and so had Martin. Perhaps he is thinking about that very story now as I do.

PARTING   43

If I could I would have told Martin my own story. I heard it first from one of my speech teachers. I would ask Martin if what happened was technically possible. I suspect it isn't, that what I have is another tale. But it is satisfying in some ways, especially when the wife comes to say good-bye. What would she say? Her husband alive somehow but two grain hoppers coupled right through him in such a way, so tightly, my teacher said, that his insides are all packed in, his organs shoved up into his chest. There is so much violence suspended between those cars, and his legs are up off the ground. And so much loneliness, too, because he is still alive. I suppose there is shock, unconsciousness, if you can believe it at all. But the redemption, the reason I think of this, is that the man's wife works in an office near the tracks and the trainmen go and fetch her.

When I think about the story I think about the trainmen rushing in, the type clatter stopping, the women pivoting in their chairs. I think about the wife grabbing her purse from back of the big file drawer on the lower left-hand side of her desk. When I heard the story first, they held her by the elbows. She stood on her tiptoes, whispered in her husband's ear. What? Good-bye. There was steam and the bulk of the steel, its chill atmosphere, and way off the thrumming engine, the engineer trying not to make a move. This was supposed to have happened in Decatur, Indiana, in the Central Soya yards. My teacher worked there in the summers, picked up the story on a coffee break, told it to me years later after a lesson. If it were true, what would she have said? Could he speak at all? It would be too difficult, probably out of breath, in shock. He would know what was happening. There would be that look in his eyes if they were open, the privacy, the inarticulateness of death. And then later, much later, after the wife had been led away, they'd have to separate the cars, separate what's left of him from the cars. I can see the conductor, those mule-skinner gantlets, waving the all-clear signal.

The all-clear signal.

❖

I was finally a very good baseball player. I batted left-handed. My father hid himself during the games in the lilac bushes bordering the park. There he smoked and tried not to watch me play. The bees circled above him in the flowers, the leaves. I was in the hole. I was on deck. He was nervous, I imagine, superstitious, embarrassed perhaps. Here I begin thinking of those microscopic pictures of chromosomes tearing themselves apart in cell nuclei, now it looks like iron filings lining up on a yellow piece of paper. Magnets are beneath the paper and the slivers of metal are repelling, pulling away from each other. I was some half of him.

And there was grace. To swing left-handed, to hit the ball, to run were all one motion, the weight flowing from the left side of the body to the right as the foot steps into the pitch, then on a stride closer to first base, running, running.

And as I type this I realize, too, a slight advantage to that left hand. My *a*'s and *e*'s are strong clear strikes, no ghost images, no *z* floats below the line, the weak pinkie finger simultaneously hitting the big shift key. And the return, the big chrome spoon on this Royal manual, the twisted lever was made for the heel of my left hand. The return is effortless.

The return.

The return.

I remember the little boys out in the field in their baggy uniforms, the scratchy cotton overwashed, before the synthetic fabrics. The green grass and the redwood red outfield fence, snow fence that was rolled up at the end of the season, leaving an arch of tall uncut grass, a record of the summer. Those boys chattered insectlike while the pitcher thought on the mound. How to write it? Hey-bay. Hey-bay. Hey-bay. Swing batter swing batter swing batter swing. Fire hard fire hard. All one word. Seesawing and singing, building to the pitch and starting after it from nothing. And I was in the batter's box, the catcher chanting, the fielders babbling, none of it making sense. A stutter everywhere around me. I liked the sound of it. Its patterns. Its cadence. Its life.

❖

At Breezeway we slowed and settled out from the turnpike, trying to read the yellow ticket with the boxes of numbers, the entrances and exits, and the tiny map of the road. We stalled at the booth trying to make the change.

There was still the trip through Western Maryland then and one of the redundant roads that stretches from Baltimore to Washington. The trip was nothing but an excuse.

We wound up saying good-bye in that unlucky city, in Metro Center, where there is no place to sit and all the subway lines — red, blue, yellow, green — come together. Martin was on his way to work nearby. Above. I would go on to National Airport — I had my bag — and take one of those planes that shoots straight up in the air over the Potomac, that gets out of there fast, the whole trip home in silence, suspended, known by heart.

Along the edge of the platform green lights begin to pulse when the train approaches. Air begins to flow through the station. On some other level I can hear the doorbell warning of a departing train.

I remember the therapists counting the words in the sentences I spoke, long columns of numbers on the charts. I remember them waiting for me to finish, to be sure that the pause was a period. That there was a thought completed. They were trying to determine my mean length of utterance. Just how long could I go before ruin, decay, explosion, waste, disappearance, silence. They weren't really listening to me, to what was being said, but to its ending, the harmonics of closure, that falling off in voice. And I would want to string it out, add and digress both. It was no good.

This is the way I said good-bye to Martin. I could not have said good-bye in any other way, in any way that would make sense to you.

Martin rose out of the station on moving stairs to his desk, where a man is broken on the dry blue bottom of a motel swimming pool, where the whole office is inhaling the lethal fumes of correction, white-out.

I have another friend who has made an anatomical gift on the back of his driver's license. He is giving only his lips. The card is laminated. My friend loves to think of his death. The police trying to make heads or tails out of it. Doctors being told of the donation. My friend thinks of the harvest of his body, his smile.

As I type I am concentrating, forming the words with my lips: Flesh. And blood. And metal. And light.

THE THIRD DAY
OF TRIALS

Intake

In the back of the motor home, the men played euchre loudly, trumping quickly and tossing in the hand after the first two plays. Phil and Bill Erhman looked like bowers themselves, one full-face, one profile. They were not partners at the table and argued over a loner and the number of points allowed. They were in the asphalt business, entertaining clients today, contractors mostly or state highway inspectors. Whenever the motor home hit a new patch of pavement or a new stretch of concrete on the interstate, they would all start up, listening.

"Shhh. Shhh. Shhh." Phil would say, concentrating on the pitch of the tires. "Marion. Marion, Indiana." And someone would look out the window, and there we would be, passing Marion, Indiana.

My father, sitting across the tiny galley table from me, was explaining something about football with coins, all heads up and vibrating from the road.

"The belly series," he said, "depended upon everyone doing the same thing every time, every play. Faking is the same as carrying the ball. Always covering the belly." My father had played football with the Erhmans on the 1952 mythical state champion team of Indiana. Father had been the quarterback of the full-house backfield. The Erhmans were the halfbacks. The fullback, A. C. Russian, was in prison.

"One game I started limping after each play as I carried out my fake," Father said. "Watching the end every play, sooner or later, I lulled him to sleep. He forgot about me. He thought I was really hurt. And on the next play I kept the ball, put it on my hip, and rolled right around him." He scooted the dime toward me with his index finger.

We traveled down the interstate from Fort Wayne to Indianapolis. We hit a bad bit of road and a hollow ringing bridge. "Muncie," Phil shouted from the back, and there was Armick's Truck Stop. Its lights were gravy-colored through the tinted window. Many trucks squeezed together in the lot, lights out, exhausts idling. It was still early.

This was the second weekend of time trials, the third day of the Indianapolis 500. Father took this trip every year with his friends. They started with a party the night before and left early in the morning. They continued to drink, tell stories, and do business. The Erhmans like to sell asphalt at night, when the patching and puckering of the road was invisible. We had to stand up in the motor home every time we passed over a section of the road they had paved so that we could feel it through our feet. "Take your shoes off. Walk around." After last year's major accidents at the track, they hoped to place a bid with the management to resurface the whole course. Father had nothing to do with the business but went along for the ride. To see the trials.

"On the third day of trials someone is on the bubble," he said. "That's why I like the third day because of the bubble. That means, usually, the whole field is filled up and the bumping starts. The slowest qualifying time from the first weekend is on the bubble. If someone goes faster his bubble bursts. He gets bumped out of place just like that. You want a beer?"

It was barely light by the time we reached Indianapolis. We took the sweeping banked curve with the John Deere dealership nestled behind it. The green and yellow tractors became visible. The ground around showed black, recently disked — a demon-

SAFETY PATROL

stration. The one banked curve on the straight highway antici-
pated the city.

"A two-stroke engine has a baffle. Have you ever heard an un-
muffled engine?" my father asked. "Really?"

I had lived in Indianapolis for a while. In those moments when
the whole city became quiet in the late afternoon, when the
various oscillations of noise matched their pulses of hills and
valleys, in the small depressions of silence, I could hear the yawn
of an engine coming from the track and the tatter of a loud-
speaker voice drifting after it. That would be the tire tests.
Spring.

"I taught you your left and right in a car. The left hand was
where the steering wheel was. The oncoming traffic messed you
up again. All the daddys were on the wrong side. Fooled you."

The motor home eased on to an exit ramp, kept left and
looped over the top of the highway. It then descended upon and
merged with 465, belted around the whole city. Going east. The
wrong way. The long way. The track was on the west side of
town. This was done every year, too, a trip taken every year all
the way around the city. A parade lap. The motor home wal-
lowed back and forth between the four lanes, jockeying for no
reason, responding slowly as things came up. The Erhmans
lapsed into a spiel on slurry and expansion coefficients. We
swayed by the first Steak-'n'-Shake drive-in, black and white, a
shadow in the bell of a trumpet exchange. The striped awnings of
the restaurant were already down in the new light, and a boy in
white was on a ladder changing light bulbs in the sign that read
dimly, In Sight It Must Be Right.

"When you were little I took you to every one of Don Hall's
drive-ins," my father whispered. "Each time he had a son, Don
Hall put up another drive-in. He gave them all names. His sons
and his restaurants. Both the same names. Trying to get both of
them right. The Hollywood next to the Roller Dome. The
Stockyard. The Old Gas House. The Factory. The Prime Rib.
Imagine, Prime Rib Hall. The Lantern. You had one of those car
seats with the little plastic wheel. It had a little mousey horn. The
parking lots were flocked with pigeons pecking crumbs."

We panned around the sun and slingshot to the south, snapped

black cloud suspended in the haze of dust and exhaust. I hold my scarf up to my mouth, filtering my breath through the wool scented with unburned gasoline. In my head, I conjugate the winners with the races as I trot beside my father through the corridor to the ramp, descend, detouring through the exhibition hall downstairs, makeshift pits, where the midgets are being loaded on the trailers. Some are being pushed up ramps; others are running up on their own power. The trailers are hooked up to pickups with their engines running, blending together in an anxious idle. Someone touches a butterfly and then lets go as we turn. He still wears a sooty balaclava and metallic fire suit. One-third the size of the old front-engine Offys, the midgets pack up like grips, a roll bar no bigger than a handle, the decals on the cowling like those old travel stamps on steamer trunks — Champion, Monroe, STP, Goodyear, Hurst, Fram, Borg-Warner, Bell. Chains ratchet through axles. Tailgates slam, and lights come on. A truck guns and stalls and starts again. They will drive all night tonight and race tomorrow in Kokomo. We head for the doors.

Outside in the dark parking lot, the air is cold and empty. Father revs up the car and goes on and on about the way they turned *into* the skid, coaxes the car into gear and slips into the nearest street. As we slow for the first light, a pickup with a trailer coasts by. It enters the intersection as the light turns red, hits the bump at the crest of the cross street, and gives a little flip, like a fluke, as it eases down the grade on the far side and is gone in the night. Once more, because we are not moving, things begin to thicken, and the car closes in. Everything that usually escapes invisibly draws together in steam and smoke, finally heaves into a body, takes another breath, and disappears.

Power

In the trunk of my father's car there was a Polaroid camera with packets of black-and-white film, striped with bands of gray to distinguish them from color packages. There was chalk in boxes marked like crayon boxes but pale and faded. The chalk dust powdered everything, messed in with the grease of the folded tar and feathered jacks. There were tape measures as big as plates, with foldaway handles, purple snap lines in tear-shaped canisters, rolls of masking tape, black tarry electrician's tape on spools, and white medical tape in unopened tubes. On the first-aid kit was a green cross, and Father used an identical but empty kit for his toolbox, which he also kept in the trunk with jumper cables and two spare tires. A bright-red cartridge fire extinguisher for A, B, and C fires, and flares in red paper, rolled orange warning flags and reflectors. And a twenty-five pound bag of lime. "For the weight," he said, "in winter."

Once, when I was little, we went to a Hall's drive-in, and I used the ledge above the back seat as a table. I spilled my drink, and it drained into the trunk through the rear radio speaker. The speaker shorted; the voice gargled out beneath the paper napkins and foil I was using to blot up the mess. Father was already outside, the trunk lid up and the car rocking up and down gently, as he slid the things around with a hiss that was transmitted by the metal of the car. I watched him through the crack left between the body and the open lid. He wiped up the drink as it dripped down and mixed with the chalk dust, smearing the floor. He checked his equipment and then rearranged it. Satisfied, he slammed the trunk lid back down, and it caught on the first time for once and did not spring back up again as it usually did. He even hesitated, expecting it to pop up again. He tapped the trunk once and looked up at me in the rear window, surprised by his own strength. The car still rocked gently up and down. The pigeons circled and settled back on the ground.

Father worked as the director of safety for the phone company and used the camera and the tape measures to investigate the traffic accidents that involved the company's trucks. He spent part of every week taking pictures of wrecks, visiting accident scenes and reconstructing what had happened. At night on the dinner table, he would unroll his schematic drawings of street grids. Colored rectangles stood for cars and trucks. Sometimes he would use tokens from board games. He penciled in vectors and numbers, all done on pale-blue veined graph paper. "I know that corner," I would say. He frowned as I put a glass of milk down on a parking lot. I told him, as I chewed my sandwich, of this great crash on Spring Street or how the coral color of Jim Musbaum's Chevy at Baerfield Raceway matched the color of that car there. I pointed and smudged the picture. Father frowned again, answered that this man overdrove his headlights. Staring off, he recalled conversion tables, following distance, and reaction time. This man couldn't see and forgot about a blind spot. "He didn't honk his horn at the alley opening." Those types of things. "Don't spill," he warned.

The rest of his job concerned prevention and education. He distributed drivers' education films that always culminated in a fatality, gave tests, put warnings on windows of trucks. He modified mirrors to magnify, came up with catchy slogans such as "Look alive in '75." He also kept a black briefcase in the trunk of his car, up by the seat. Every now and then he would simulate accidents to test first-aid skills and response time of police and fire units. He used the briefcase then.

I went along one time and watched him. He had arranged for a smashed-up car to be left in a certain ditch by our house. After putting on special blood-smeared and torn clothes that he kept in his kit, he added splashes of fake blood for fresh wounds and lacerations. He put on a medical-warning bracelet that said he was allergic to sulfa drugs. To see if they would check. He then threaded a rubber tube up his sleeve and taped it to his arm. At the other end of the tube was a rubber bulb like a perfume atomizer. He held the bulb close to his chest and with his free hand pumped more blood from a plastic bag he wore suspended from his neck. The blood went through the tube and out the other end, where it spurted like a severed artery at his wrist. In his kit, he had plastic casts he could strap on a leg or arm which approximated simple, compound, or complex fractures. He had ace bandages that had been treated to look like burns, first to third degree.

He wedged himself through the broken windshield of the car, careful not to cut himself on the exposed sheet metal, and tucked his legs under the collapsed dash. Appearing to be pinned, he affected the shallow breathing of shock. His hand out the window, he tried a test beat or two from his wound and it squirted, a trick plastic flower on a lapel.

"How do I look?" he asked.

"Pretty bad," I answered truthfully.

"Good, good. Go call those numbers."

I left him there and went to a phone booth to call the police and the company's own emergency squad. By the time I returned, I could hear the sirens coming up the by-pass. I stood a little way off and looked at my father slouched and unconscious. A red trickle bled down the car door. The shadow his hair cast darkened his forehead. A rear tire had sprung a leak, and the car was settling slowly. His finger twitched.

Passing cars slowed down. Some stopped, pulled off to the side. Passengers got out and ran up to the car. There were sirens now. Someone was directing traffic. The police and the ambulance pulled up. I went closer and saw some police clearing the area, explaining to those who tried to help. They thanked them, but there was nothing anyone could do. The emergency crews cut away the door with a gasoline-powered tool that shook the car and sounded like a chain saw. My father's head rolled back and forth on the seat. Someone bent over and yelled in his ear. Someone else was holding the bleeding wrist. On the other side of the car, they broke out the window, trying to free him that way. There were more sirens now, called by passing motorists, and a television crew that must have been in the area, listening to the police band. Father was on the ground, and they could not stop the bleeding. They were bringing blankets. A man's hand was streaked red between the fingers. There was a scratch on my father's earlobe just flushed with blood. A piece of glass must have caught him when they broke the window. I could see him stretched out on the ground through the legs of people standing around. A wrecker pulled up. Its brakes coming on and a radio playing. Another man stood up from where he had been crouching over my father. There was no more blood. Someone pronounced him dead and laughed shortly, pulling back the blankets and wiping his hands on my father's shirt.

Exhaust

When we passed the sign near Penalton which warns against picking up hitch-hikers because the penitentiary is so close, the motor home slowed and pulled over. The Ehrmans led everyone out the two doors, and we lined up along the drainage ditch and faced in the direction of the prison. The prison water tower was silhouetted now and then by the sweeping searchlights. Low to the ground and this far away, not much else could be seen. The men started to shout.

"Come on out, Russian," and "Now's your chance." Between each chorus, they would pause to listen, then huddle, deciding on what to say next. Lining up again, my father would pace them, "one, two, three," directing with his hands.

"We're waiting."

A Funk Seed Hybrid sign was on the fence by the road. The cornfield was empty. There was not even an echo.

"He's not coming," someone said, and we got back in.

Starting up the road again my father said that it was a shame I had to see a year of trials when turbine cars were entered. "I miss the sound," he said. He waved his head as if following an imaginary vehicle from left to right and pursed his lips together to imply a sound, because that was what the new engines did. Imply a sound.

We stopped one more time that night. A few miles from home, we pulled off into a closed weigh station. I got out and climbed the ladder to the roof of the motor home. The siding was cold as I sat down under the TV antenna cocked like a café umbrella. Across the highway was an identical station. It was closed, too. Beyond that was a barn. Showing in the circle of the mercury light was the name of the place, Belle Acres, painted below a smiling image of the Good Sam Club that spotted the dark barn, a hex sign. Good Sam smiled broadly, eyes bugging, his halo tilted back out of the way.

My father and his friends were running races up and down the driveway. They ran heats, two or three men at a time. Someone sat at the finish line with a folding TV table and campstool keeping score. As they ran, their shadows spiraled around their feet, scooting between the pools of light.

Father ran easily, won his heat, slowed down way beyond the finish line, then turned and limped back up the apron. I applauded alone until I was interrupted by a car honking its horn as it went by on the interstate. I turned to wave. A new race started. Father, passing on his way back to the starting line, looked up at me and jerked his head from left to right performing the first half of a double take, pretending to hum along as the silent racer passed before his eyes. He hobbled back up the drive toward the hut, where his friends were jumping up and down on the scale. He bent over now and then to catch his breath.

They ran a few more heats until the man at the TV table fell asleep and put his head on his hands. The Erhmans led a walking tour north toward home, examining shoulder material. As they began to sing, they disappeared into the night.

Father and I went back inside the motor home and started up the engine, waiting for them to return. More and more trucks appeared on the highway. The sky paralleled the black field, leaving a space in between. He listened to a horn blasting down the road and to the engine beneath our feet. "Something's missing," he said, swiveling in the captain's chair. He talked until the engine died, out of gas, fitting word into word until I finished sentences he had started. I could no longer tell where we were by the sound the night was making. But by then it didn't matter; we had been carried on, by the dead center, to where it already was the next day.

WATCH OUT

My Story

I will write my story using English only, as my students should
do. I will write about our new home and how we live. I will write
about the class I teach and my very good students who will read
this and who are pleased to be here in Indiana. There is the
church to write about too and our Bishop Leo. But most of all I
will write in English about learning it and not using my own
tongue or French because we are here now and must learn this
one way to talk.

Things You Must Know

I am a woman. I am five feet high. My Christian name is
Catherine. In my country, I lived with the Sisters of the Sacred
Heart and the Sisters of the Most Precious Blood and I remember
the white, black, and gray colors of their clothes and how hot it
must have been. With them, I learned French and English and the
ways to teach others these languages. I worked hard and had a
good time. My hair is black. My eyes too. I can drive a car. I can
run a typewriter. I was afraid, of course, when I came to Amer-

ica. But with the help of the Diocese of Fort Wayne–South Bend and the Fort Wayne Community Schools everything is fine now. I have no family in this country, but I have a father, a mother, two brothers, a sister, two uncles and their wives who are my aunts, and several cousins. All of my grandparents are no longer living.

My Health Problem

In America there is food. In America there are all kinds of food. When I arrived in America there were signs everywhere that said Eat. But when I came here to this country with all this food, I cannot eat. The food looks like wood and tastes like mud to me. Even the food of my country that we make here no longer tastes good to me now. I lose so much weight that my boss, Mrs. Anthis, is startled each time she sees me. She pretends everything is fine, but I can see.

Where I Work

I work for the public schools under a title from the President of the United States. "We are lucky to find you," Mrs. Anthis says. This is after she pretends not to worry about me. "We were lucky to find her," she says to her bosses when I am introduced to them. These men are kind and they want to shake my hand all the time. They don't know much about my country except for the war and they don't talk about that. They say, "Why, you are so little!" I laugh. I teach English to the children of my country so that they can go to regular school one day. Everyone knows America is the land of opportunity. Here is an example.

Where We Live

Our Bishop Leo lets us live in the Central Catholic High School. Let me tell you that it is not a high school now with students and teachers. It is called CC. There are other high schools where Catholic boys and girls go to learn. Those schools are far away, on the edge of the city. Many families live here. We are waiting to find houses of our own and for the children without families to be adopted. We have made curtains for the big windows at CC. The lights are tubes filled with gas. They hum. There are many places for the children to hide. They hide in the old desks. They run down the halls and hide in the lockers in the wall. Often they will jump out at me as I walk by. There is a gym and a greenhouse on the roof where people have planted seeds they brought with them. Each family has a classroom of its very own. I live in the room with many sewing machines, refrigerators, sinks, and ovens. It was decided that it would be best if I lived here since I am alone. Now, no woman with a family will be jealous of another. Each family has its own oven and a place to put food. Water is in this room, so the washing is done here too. It dries on the roof. There are smells of cooking in my room and much laughter among the women. It is okay because I work in school in the days and on the days I don't work I talk to the children or take them to places so they will hear English. There is a room of typewriters, too. I am there now. Every room has a clock on the wall. The thin hand is always moving. My room is quiet at night but for the refrigerators. I think to myself that they talk to one another. I hear the bells of the churches every fifteen minutes, and I hear the pigeons near the windows making their soft noises.

The Churches of Fort Wayne

There are many beautiful and interesting churches in the city. Many of the churches are near downtown, and we walk to them to hear daily mass. Sometimes we travel to the churches farther away, taking the black cars of the priests. Then we meet the people there in the new churches. We sit in the front pews with ushers standing by. The people talk to us slowly and give us boxes of cans. These are the new churches where there are many people and where they wear bright clothes and the ceilings are low and sparkle. I am thinking of St. Jude's and St. Vincent's, where the statues are smooth wood and never painted. Near to CC are the old churches. There is the cathedral of our Bishop Leo. It is called Immaculate Conception. There the stations of the cross are twice as big as life and there are banks of votive candles kept burning by the older people. There are side altars. The building is white and Mary has a crown of pure gold on her head. We have heard stories about a workman who caught on fire and fell burning from the steeple we can see from our windows at CC but lived. Nearby is a big rock where the Indians converted. There is St. Mary's made out of red sandstone. It is a church built in the old way. There are bats that live here high up near the painted ceiling. There is St. Peter and St. Paul, which is made with red brick. There is St. Patrick with one steeple. There is Precious Blood, which has two steeples and beautiful bells. There is Queen of the Angels, which is in an old gym since they are so poor. There is colored paper in the windows. And there is a shrine to the Virgin near the wrecking yard and power plant where the orphanage is and near the place where football is played. Near to CC is a chapel. It is open all the time. But someone must be there praying day and night. You can see the body of Christ. There it is in the center of a golden cross inside a round window. I go to this chapel often to hear mass at noon with the workers from the banks who are not having dinner. The chapel might not remain open at night. People are afraid to be alone in the early morning. I have spent many happy hours visiting these places and talking to the friendly people.

Worry

I believe I am not doing a very good job. This happens when the children call out the windows of CC at Americans on the street. The children use their own language and slam the windows. They do not want to leave the building but play games in the hallway near the glass cases that have old awards for sports. They play near the fountains and waste water. I speak to them in English and they don't understand. I know they know some English but they are afraid too. They do not want Americans to lose patience with them. They try to tell me how things are, but I shake my head. "Say it in English, please!" If I were bigger, I could do a better job.

In the Classroom

When they are not working, the parents of my students visit the classroom. They sit in the little chairs with the children on their laps. Or they sit next to the children on the floor and try to read the simple English. Then I hear them asking the children what this word is or what that one is. And I hear the children say the word in the old language. *Ball* or *dog*. I don't feel so bad then. The parents tell me it is too late for them to learn. Then they fall into silence. Then they tell the children to try harder. I say, "Let's sing a song!" With the children singing it is very nice and everyone is happier.

At CC I Am Very Busy

We all wait for the mail to come in the big bags brought by a man in a truck. People want me to read to them the letters that have come in English. Often these letters suggest buying things such as records, magazines, spoons, seeds, and food. There are other letters from leaders. Once a week, our Bishop Leo writes. And I read the *Sunday Visitor* for everyone when we all eat together. There are papers to fill out for others. And I talk to the operator when the family heads are called in other cities. I write notes for the men to take to the bank with their checks. On Sunday when Father Hamilton says mass in the little chapel, I translate the words for him. It makes me very happy to help.

Sunday Brunch

Mrs. Anthis took me to a Sunday brunch. She wanted to put meat on my bones. The Sunday brunch was at a restaurant owned by Mr. Hall. Many of the men from CC wash dishes there. There was much to eat. Bacon, ham, beef, chicken, fish, lamb, sausage, and eggs which were fried, scrambled, boiled, and eggs made a special way and given names. There was fruit. Apples, oranges, grapes, cherries, bananas, pineapples, berries, grapefruit, and many juices. There were potatoes with onions that were sliced or in long strips. There were breads that were sweet and had icing, and cakes, and bread in paper, and loaves of bread with three types of butter, one that had strawberries inside it. There was honey, and syrup for pancakes, and yellow corn bread. You could drink all the coffee you wanted. You could go back to the food tables as many times as you liked. People walked around the big room with two plates. Mrs. Anthis said, "This is our favorite place." Her husband was there and her children and other teachers. Some of the men from CC waved to me when no one else was looking. They were carrying dishes from the tables. "No wonder," Mrs. Anthis said, "Are you sure you don't want anything more?" she said. I was listening to all the English in the room, and that was enough for me.

I Become Sicker

I have gone again to the doctor. He wears a white coat, and there are folds at the bottom of his pants. There are bars on the windows, and the table where I sit is covered by a thin piece of white paper. The sister pulls out a new piece of paper from the end of the table. She pulls it tight and shiny. I am always afraid to sit on this new piece of paper and put wrinkles into it. I remember the women at CC with the hot irons and the steam and the stiff legs of their husbands' checkered pants. The women go back and forth with irons. "Go on. Sit down. It's only paper," the sister says. "You must eat," the doctor says. "Why don't you eat?" But I don't have the words to tell him why. They both look at me and I am so afraid. My hand goes back and forth on the paper. Then I cut my finger on the edge of the paper. There is some blood on the white paper and we are all surprised.

Downtown

The children are like sparrows. We go downtown and they run and follow one another. They all land at one spot. They all look into the mirror the Murphy's has on their building, and then they fly, one after another, to the boxes that have newspapers. We are about the only people downtown. The people work in offices high up in the tall buildings. The children like to stop in front of the wig shop. In the window of the wig shop are black heads with all different kinds of hair that shines in the light. Most store windows are painted white and have old signs that say Closed. The clocks have stopped on the store signs. In the street I see where a railroad track has been covered over by new paving. This city is so different from the old cities. The children run from one place to another. There are only big green buses in the streets. Without the buses the streets would be empty. "Where are the people?" the children ask. "Say it in English," I say. "Hiding! They're hiding!" the children say. The children are jumping at a string of lights in a small tree without leaves. "They are up there, the people, in all of those windows. They are speaking English to one another." That is what I say to them.

In Another Classroom

I have been to the Catholic high schools to talk to students there. I tell them stories like these about what we do and how we live and about my students. Mrs. Anthis stands in the back of the room and smiles. After awhile, a bell rings and the students collect their books from the little shelves under their chairs. They go. And new students come in and sit down. I say the same things about Fort Wayne and the beautiful churches and the children and CC and the green buses. The students listen closely. They smile and look at each other. They listen hard to me. They look hard at me. I feel as if I am talking softer and softer, and I am afraid that I have not said something I said before to another class. "What, dear?" Mrs. Anthis says. "What is it?" And I can't explain with these students watching me.

The Children's Zoo

The zoo of Fort Wayne has only young animals. There are the cubs of lions and monkeys and bears and kangaroos. There are baby elephants and turtles and pigs. Everywhere there are the chicks of birds scratching the ground. The small rabbits live in a big shoe. In one building, many tiny snakes, like noodles, were under an orange light wrapped around and around each other on a bed of sawdust. My students and I rode a small train around a lake. We went into a yard where kids and lambs ran after us and sucked our fingers until we gave them bottles of milk. I pointed and called every animal by name. I told the children that the zoo was a place for children. The grown-up animals must go to other zoos. "These animals you can play with now." And my students rubbed the fur and held the animals tight, and then they tried to carry the animals away while the animals made such loud crying noises. We fed the seals also. We bought food from a machine like the candy machines at CC. I pulled on a handle and the food arrived. The noise we made with the machine was heard by the seals, and they came up out of the cold green water onto the rocks and sang as their fur dried in the sun. The children threw food to them through the air, and the heads of the seals and their long necks moved back and forth following the food as it fell.

Our Country Will Not Go Away

Near CC is a garden enclosed in glass so that the flowers and the trees will grow even in the winter. All of us love to go there on Sunday after mass. The first room changes with the seasons. Pine trees grow there at Christmas. Lilies grow there at Easter. In the fall, there is colored corn and on the floor are leaves. Sometimes there are only tulips and roses. The next room is a desert, and it is filled with stones and bushes. It is very dry, and the plants are small. We must look for them but there are bright red flowers in the thorns. The last room is like our home. There is a mist shooting from the glass roof, and there is the sound of water everywhere. There is the smell in the mud. The roots of the trees wrap back up around the trunks and soon become the trunk. The leaves are big and dark green and heavy with water. The little stream is green. There is rice in the paddy and the bamboo is thick. The men talk to each other and point at how this or that plant has grown. The women watch the waterfall. The children, in their good clothes, sleep under the trees. Goldfish float in the pools. I read the small red signs and look for one that says this plant is from our home. I live to breathe in and out in this place. It would be great to live only by breathing.

One Night

One night the children were crying. Outside it was snowing, and the trucks that never stop were going by the building. The windows shook in the wind. The air in my room was hot and dry. It was very dark. I heard the children cry. The children were in their rooms and their crying came in under the door of my room. Then I heard mothers and fathers awake. The voices were low and they sang songs. It was like being rocked again by my mother's voice so far away. It was so hot and dry in my room. I wanted to move my bed to the floor. There near the ground would be cool air. I took off my nightshirt, which was red and pretty. I got it from the people of the church we visited. When I pulled the nightshirt over my head, I saw a flash of light. The light ran around my body and arms and legs and fingers and into my hair. Every time I moved there were more sparks and a sound like sitting on the paper in the doctor's office. The light was blue and green and it did not hurt. When I shook my head against my nightshirt there would be more sparks. I watched this for a long time. And that is why the children cried. One child woke that night and saw the light playing on the bodies of his mother and father and sisters and his brothers as they turned in bed against the sheets and blankets. He was frightened and called out. When everyone woke up and moved in the bed there was more light flashing in the dark and they thought they were on fire and cried for help. The next family woke up and the same thing happened. Then everyone was awake and screaming for help. But it was nothing. It was the new clothes, something in the new clothes, that made this happen. The women came into my room to wash the clothes in the dark.

Watch Out

The next day in class, I told the children how to ask for help in English. Help me. How to say I am hurt. I am hurt. I taught them to say be careful. Be careful. I taught them to say I am afraid. I am afraid. I taught them to say I'm scared. I'm scared. They learned the words *run, move, duck.* I told them don't look and I didn't see it and be calm and get out of the way. I taught them none of your business and leave me alone and I am okay and I can't walk. I taught the children to say I am sick. I am sick. And let me sit down and rest. Let me sit down and rest. And I can't go on. I can't go on. I taught them bad, evil, wrong, pain, and death. Yes, I told them the word for death. Death. And I said, "Watch out." "Say it. Watch out." "You say it now," I said. I said, "Watch out." And the children said, "Watch out." I said, "That's good." And the children said, "Watch out! Watch out!" as loud as they could.

In the Middle of Another Night

I go to the small chapel to sit and think. The people who must sit there sit together away from me in one pew. They turn to look at me when they think I am not looking but praying. I think of my family. Where they are and what they must be doing because it is day on the other side of the world. And I think at times in the old language when I think of my mother and father and I pretend they can hear me like it was a prayer. When the new people come to take the place of the people who have been sitting and watching, they all turn to look at me and to whisper to each other. Then I think I am really safe here in Fort Wayne.

Later

No one is out in the downtown. There are no sounds. Nothing is open. I am not afraid to walk around. Why should I be afraid? There is no one here. I asked Mrs. Anthis this. "Why do people stay away?" And she said, "They are afraid." I said, "Afraid of what?" "Of what is downtown." I said, "Are they afraid of us?" "No, no, my dear," she said, "they are just afraid." But there is no one here but us. There is no one here at all but us. I know because I walk around at night. "You, you tiny thing?" she said. "Yes," I said. I never see anyone else. But the lights that direct the traffic still work. There are big piles of snow in the corner of the parking lots where the buildings used to be, and in the middle of the parking lots are little houses that are empty. Inside the houses, I see through the window a light is on and the cash register is open and empty. When the wind blows snow off the piles, it flows over the black ground of the empty lots like a clear shallow river, white and running fast.

A Disease

The doctor told me of a disease he thinks makes me not eat. I cried in his office sitting on the paper on his table. I cried because I am not hungry and because I am fading away to nothing. That is what the sister said when I stood on the scale. "You are fading away to nothing." I cried because I am doing something wrong. I cried because I have no one to talk to. The doctor said it was something in the air, this disease. He said that very many American girls who cannot eat are sick with it. Girls in America, he said, want to look good in bathing suits. "Do you want to look good in a bathing suit?" I cried because I had never thought of bathing suits before. The doctor can think of nothing else it can be. "That must be it," he said and then he said good-bye and left me in the little room to get dressed.

Tet

It is our first new year in America. At CC we have a party in the gym. We play records and the sound comes out of the speakers in the ceiling. The children are running around the tables. Ribbons and colored paper sail along behind them when they run. Everyone is happy. We are using white paper plates for our food, the rice cakes and pork and lemon grass and milk. And Mrs. Anthis is here and Mr. Hall and all the bosses and the man who brings the mail. And our Bishop Leo is here too blessing everything. When I go up to him for a blessing I take his hand to kiss his ring and I cannot lift his hand in my two hands. He tells me to stand next to him on the stage and he asks me to tell him a phrase to say in celebration. He leans over and I tell him and he says it a few times to himself. Everyone is quiet when he speaks in English and then he speaks in the old language and everyone cheers. And our Bishop Leo says I am a good teacher. And I look at the faces. They are eating and drinking. They do not understand what has been said and they are waiting for me to translate, to say that I am a good teacher. But I say in the old language that all of you are my family, that we are here together, one body, and that we must eat all the food and not waste a bit of it.

In Another Building

We went to the top of one of the tall buildings. My students ran through the empty restaurant that is there. They ran from one big window to another and looked down carefully at the city. The restaurant was closed, so we could come in and see and not trouble anybody. Windows were everywhere and they were so big it seemed you could walk right out into the sky. Outside we saw the steeples of the churches and the green rivers way off in the distance. Below we saw the tops of the green buses and the parking lots filled with cars. We saw CC below us and the washing on the roof. Below us too were many gray pigeons flying together from one building to another. And the children asked quietly in the old language where the people were now, and I tried to show them the houses all around. But the trees made everything disappear. And the children said, "They're hiding. They're hiding." Some men from CC who work in this place were putting knives and forks and spoons on the table. The metal made a pretty sound. The children stood very close to the windows all in a line looking out. The lights of the houses and cars came on like stars in the sky. And with us in the sky, the stars began to show up. I could smell the food in the kitchen and I told everyone it was time to go. There were more and more lights all around the city, long straight lines of lights where the roads were. Why should I be this lucky one in America?

AN ACCIDENT

The train would be gone by the time he got to the scene. The train had been late this morning. That might mean something. After this it would be very late into Chicago.

He drove at the speed limit. There was no radio. It was a company car.

The railway paralleled U.S. 30 between Fort Wayne and Warsaw. Conrail wanted to abandon the route. The waves in the telegraph line flattened out where an insulator had popped free of the pole, a green clot floating there in the taut wire.

It was the day after Labor Day. It was clear and bright. There had been no fog that morning in the low-lying areas. The leaves were still on the trees. The corn was tall and green in the fields. All of this could be important.

His wife wrote up the reports at the kitchen table. He did not take notes at the accidents he investigated for the company but presented the facts to her, the way he remembered them, while he ate. Rarely did he draw conclusions. She asked leading questions, partly because the forms demanded certain connections be made, partly because she was curious and thought best with a pencil in her hand. Once she got started it was hard for her to stop.

70

Both of them had forgotten when it was he had stopped writing. They never talked about it. He never had written much. But now he felt awkward scribbling down a phone number. He had been embarrassed when the company had given him a Cross pen and pencil set upon his promotion from craft to the safety department.

The firemen were still putting water on the truck. He judged it to be about two thousand feet from the grade crossing. The train was gone.

The driver of the truck, pronounced dead on the scene, had been taken to Fort Wayne though his home was nearby. The crossing was in a little town called Atwood and only had lights, no gate. The passenger train doesn't stop there. Its next stop is Whiting, the last stop before Chicago.

He heard the figures of 242, 312 and 276 people on board. He had talked to the other investigators there. They had given him the numbers but not what they thought about them. There were state troopers, a deputy sheriff from the county, some men from OSHA, a man from Conrail, a man from Amtrak, the railroad's insurance man and Amtrak's insurance man, the company's insurance man. The man who was killed, his insurance man. And he was here now. There were several witnesses, too, standing around talking to each other.

He stood for a second at the crossing. He saw a whistle warning, a capital *W* in the Pennsylvania keystone. The crossing was wood, splintered and bleached. A blacktop led up to it. The rails were bright, not rusted. Two tracks and a siding, unused, making for a deserted elevator. The ballast was weathered and oil-stained. There was the diesel smell and the smell of urine dumped on the tracks from the toilets of the old passenger cars Amtrak still used. A date nail dated the last maintenance to seven years ago. The creosote was gray and hard and some ties were gouged.

A column of smoke coiled up from the tires of the truck two thousand feet away. Some flares sputtered up the track. A torpedo had been left behind by the train crew and, beyond where the white rails came together, a lone signal block hovered above the track and the heat, showed red.

Along both rails was pure white sand. It started a little before the crossing and burrowed by the rails to where the train came to

AN ACCIDENT 71

rest and where the truck slid down the elevation and burned. It was fine, powder, and felt, when he walked on it, like sand-blasting sand at the foot of a building. It was the same grade of sand. The same used in a kid's playground.

His wife would conclude that the train came to a gradual halt. The engineer knew he had killed the man in the truck when he hit it, had sanded freely and braked slowly at the same time, looking down on the yellow truck sliding ahead of him. The fireman was already out the cab door and out on the rail steps. The truck started to burn in the rear. Ladders spilled from the racks on its roof. There would be a big pile of sand where the engine came to rest. The passengers would have to be told what had happened. The deceleration would have felt ordinary. The train was late. What now? The conductor put the radio mike to his mouth. "Amtrak 41."

Her husband told her the speed limit was fifty-nine miles per hour and that he was probably going about that. Say sixty. The engine was painted silver with red, blue, and white striping. Two headlights and two blue strobe lights are to be on the lead unit. The fire in the truck scorched the engine's sides. Someone had to pay for that.

It was the day after Labor Day. The train was westbound from New York and Washington to Chicago. It was late. Usually it passed through Atwood around a quarter after six each morning. Today it was eight thirty-five when the truck was hit. This he got from a retired railway man who lived by the tracks.

"Did you hear the horn?" he asked him.

"Yes, I heard it."

"Once? Twice? What?"

"I heard it twice. It wasn't the engineer's fault."

"No one else says they heard it."

"I heard it. They're wrong."

"Not once?"

"Twice."

The track here runs due west. The truck crossed north to south. The sun would have been to the left of the driver. The train rising in the east.

He watched the men go about their jobs. Two of them, using a cloth tape measure, measured the distance, stretching out the tape to its full length, and then one ran by the other, stretching out the tape again in relays. Another man rolled a wheel meter. It looked like a toy. One man wrote out his notes using the roof of his car, the revolving light revolving, the light washed out in the sun. The cars and trucks were yellow, orange, red, bright blue, a two-toned brown. Company colors. The radios were patched through the siren speakers and the voices flat, spitting, bitten off. From time to time he heard a bird make a sound like the sound the metal ball makes in a spray-paint can.

There had been another company truck trailing behind the one that was hit. The driver of the second truck sat in the cab, parked. The warning lights were flashing.

He said to the driver, "Backing accidents are what give us the most problems. You know if you could come up with a way to prevent them, you could make a fortune. Bell put out orange cones for awhile. Do you remember? But college kids stole them. The problem is, most things work for a while and then people get used to them." He said, "Most of the time it's backing up that gives you a fit."

The driver guessed so. They listened to the tick of the lights. There was a spray of rust in the yellow panel of the truck. The rear tires were snow tires.

"What did you see?"

"I saw the taillights, and I saw him look both ways. I saw him through the rear-door window."

"Left, right, left? What? Right, left, right?"

"The other way I think. But he was across the tracks already, still looking. I didn't see the train until it run into him and then just the aluminum and the windows. It was like a cartoon except the end of the train slowed down and I could see the faces. That's when I got out. I didn't hear the horn or anything. My engine runs fast until it's warmed up, and we had just come out from that restaurant over there and breakfast. We were in no hurry to work. I have orders for a splice down 30. And he didn't try to beat it across. I don't think he saw it. I didn't see it. He must of crossed here five or six times a day. If you ask me, those signal poles are too far from the crossing."

He asked the lineman if he would put that down in writing, handed him the folded forms.

AN ACCIDENT

The lineman said, "I'm not so good with these things."

He told him to do his best. People would understand. "That's all I do anymore." He told him to send the forms in the company mail.

Standing a little ways off were a few other men wanting to talk with the lineman. They wore ties. Two wore beepers on their belts. The other had his in his shirt pocket. The beepers were leased from the phone company. During the day a beeper would go off, and a man would walk to the pay phone by the restaurant or get in a car and drive away.

He left the lineman, crossed the track and got in his car again. He drove over the crossing without letting up on the gas. The car bucked and rocked. He did this without his seat belt on, only remembering it when he parked the car and got out on the other side of the track.

He leaned against the side of the car and reached back through the open window for the box of cigars he kept wedged between the sun visor and the roof. At home he smoked them out in the garage or in the backyard, where he looked out over the office park next door. For hours he watched the Canada geese tear at the lawns.

Later, he watched her erase a line of writing. It was different than writing one. Then her whole body leaned into the work, her head always moving steadily over the page though her eyes remained fixed on the pencil point. When she erased, she erased one letter at a time, blowing away crumbs the color of her lips. She erased completely, never leaving ghosts of letters between or under words. She held the pencil the same way as she did when she wrote. She sat at the dining-room table. The leaf leaned against the wall. The pencil sharpener stuck to the table by means of a vacuum. Each time she used it she slid her palm over the table and then blew on the rubber diaphragm under the base of the sharpener. She set it down, worked it like a brick, and flipped the lever. It held fast. He watched her work. While she wrote, the sharpener slowly let go of the tabletop, covered with crumbs.

It was the day after Labor Day. He had spent most of the weekend watching the telethon. When he worked in craft he once had done the inside work for the telephone banks. There was a phone in every room of his house, and they all rang differently. He had cut the grass.

A Conrail truck was sliding along the track up to the crossing. It was painted blue and a yellow light flashed on the crew cab. The steel wheels jacked the truck up off the track just enough so that the rear tires could propel it along.

It stopped before the crossing, skating a bit after braking. There was no sand. The horn honked, a regular horn, and the truck crept up on to the grade, where it might have raised the steel wheels but instead kept on going smoothly up the track to where the other truck still smoldered.

He watched the other investigators scatter off the track, wave at the truck as it went by. They wore ties and hard hats. A beeper went off. He heard the door of the newspaper vending machine slam shut. A car engine started by the restaurant.

The inspection truck stopped near the wreck. Its taillights came on. Three men got out and looked down the elevation at the truck. Then, they got back in their truck and continued toward Chicago.

He talked to several witnesses who told him pretty much the same story. No one had ever seen a train hit a truck before except on TV, and those crashes were in slow motion. They all talked about how fast it had happened and how long it took the train to stop. Only the retired railroad man had heard the horn, had heard it twice. The witnesses pointed to where they had been. They told him what they had done after it was over. He gave them all his business card and they slid his in with the rest.

"I'm sorry," someone said to him.

Lunch was at the restaurant. He had chili. An OSHA man was in the booth with him having a cheeseburger and coffee. They both wore their ID badges on metal chains around their necks. The badges were flat against their ties, where they leaned into the table. It was crowded and noisy. The hard hats were on the racks by the door and on the top of the cigarette machine, along with the baby boosters.

"How can someone not see a train?" the OSHA man said. "I mean not see it when it can be seen? I mean that train was one that could be seen. The right of way had been cut back. It's a question that always plagues me. Is it a matter of concentration or what? But it's a shame, a waste. We both got better things to do. I understand there are kids. The sheriff said she took it kind of hard, but what do you expect? A train is so big and this kind of thing amazes me."

He called his wife after lunch to tell her what had happened. All the phones rang.

"I'm going to need this one in kind of a hurry since there is someone dead here."

"No, I understand. I don't mind. I like doing these things for you."

"It's a mess here," he said. "He's about a couple thousand feet down the track. I have to wait for our crew. I don't think it will be anything hard to do."

"It's all right. Did you know him?" she asked.

"I knew the name. Look, I'll tell you about it when I get home."

Whenever she finished writing and she read it to him, it never was quite right. He never would say anything to her because she would suggest he write his own damn reports. Besides, he told her everything he could remember. He went around in his mind looking through all the accidents he had been to. It was his fault, he concluded, for seeing one thing and saying another. Yes, that's it. That's good enough. Giving up.

Unless he was eating he hated sitting at a table. He told his secretary that his wife rewrote his reports so that the typing would be easy.

"How can you look at such things?" his wife asked, looking up from the yellow pad, the yellow pencil rolling over the words, her fingers spread and stretching before her on the table.

❖

The back of the truck was scorched black. The paint was blistered. Snow tires were on the truck but badly burned.

A couple of men looked through the knee-high grass and bushes of the steep bank. One of them reached down, then held up a wrench. The salvage crew had parked down the bank on the access road. They slid the big metal toolboxes down the bank and loaded them up. They formed a line and passed along boxes of extension phones one at a time. They wrapped wire, like yarn, on their arms and carried it on their bodies like ammunition.

The investigators took pictures with old instant cameras. The prints had to be timed and the picture pulled apart after it had developed.

He looked in the cab, and the others crowded around him. There was blood on the window and down the side of the door. Blood on the wheel and dashboard. Blood on the order board. The one side was caved in. The side door sprung. The fire hadn't come this far forward. There was a wire screen, which protects the driver, between the seats and the equipment. Power tools were being taken out the back.

The mirror might have blocked his sight, the whole train hidden behind it when he looked that way.

He could hear the scratches of writing all around him. It was the only sound, for no one talked. The pencils whispered to the paper.

He saw the plastic woven cushion on the floor. He saw the pictures of children, the coins on the seat. He saw the toothpick. He saw the glove compartment popped open and the maintenance papers, the maps, and the rag for the oil dipstick. There was an upright Coke can and a spilled coffee cup in the tray above the engine. The tool belt was on the dash. He saw where he had put the decal on the windshield that said Look before Backing and he saw where it had been picked at.

The writing went on around him. The different scratch of an erasure.

The men from the company carried things down the hill.

He opened the door. A few men pushed around him into the truck. They poked around beneath the seats. The horn, the turn indicator switched on, the lights. Nothing worked.

He saw the train coming, though it was a ways off. One of its headlights wobbled in its socket. There was heat coming off the rails and off the hoods of the engines and the black cars it was pulling. Soon, it sounded its horn, two notes, and the engines went up in pitch. Everyone looked up from the wreck as the train came nearer, picked up speed. The engineer turned on the bell and blew the horn again. It crawled by. The fireman waved. The brakeman was out the door, walking forward to the pilot as the engine moved forward. He looked down at the track, gave a wave. Black smoke stood up from the exhaust of the six engines, and the slack in the coupling was pulled in, echoed away through the cars. He saw the thin spray of sand at the wheels. The blue engines went by. The dynamic brakes hissed, kept the air even throughout the train. The black cars were identical except for the numbers, and the numbers were white and not that much out of sequence. There was a stutter over the joint in the rail. He counted 126 empty, empty coal hoppers. The others did, too.

A SHORT, SHORT
STORY COMPLETE
ON THESE
TWO PAGES

You should know right off how everything came out. Marsha is pregnant with her second, and she still looks great. She walks even straighter, and you can see the muscles through her clothes when she moves. She moves like she's saying the baby doesn't change things.

I saw her again right before Christmas at the mall where the company we used to work for, Reader's World, has a store. Every chance I get I go in and ask the new clerks, and they're always new, if I still work for Reader's World. When they answer, I ask, "Well, whatever happened to him?"

Marsha had her straight, I mean straight, black hair in a Cleopatra cut. It was like a helmet framing the white skin of her face. She has green eyes. She's one of the few people I look at when I'm talking to them. She wore her clothes clinging tight across her belly. No tent dress. Not an ounce of fat on her except maybe her breasts, which were getting ready, you know.

She let me put my hand on her stomach right there in the mall, and I mean to tell you, the results were tympanic. You forget how hard flesh can get.

I said we worked together for a summer at Reader's World but not in the store at the mall, which they opened later, but in an old English Village shopping center way the heck out. That store is closed now because the volume never was big enough. You should know that these places are supermarkets. There's no violin music, no cats rubbing up against your leg as you browse. The books were paperbacks. We arranged them up and down according to the author's last name in display racks that showed you every front cover, boom. The shiny things were right there in front of you. Many books were part of a series, big numbers running from the ceiling to the floor, in order, appealing to the desire to collect them all. There were calendars galore and cute bookmarks next to the cash register. I mean, things had to move, or we pulled them. In the pockets behind the books were reorder, inventory cards. We combed through those daily. When we found a title about to get dusty, boom, on the floor it went. Boxes of the things arrived every day, fresh produce.

The place was owned by the local news agency that, heretofore, had only been wholesale, stocking, well, supermarket checkouts and the rack or two at the drugstores. So they had the books. They integrated vertically.

But the main push came with magazines, and here I've got to admit it was impressive. They had, have everything, every mass-market, consumer, commercial, special-interest, slick and pulp magazine and more the bookstore ordered right from the publishers. As the only male I was hired to take care of the rack.

Marsha and I hit it off right away. The other women were much older. They popped in from tanning in their backyards to work a few hours. This is minimum-wage country, second-income city. They liked to read and talk about books with the friends who'd stop by asking if we had anything more by this one author they couldn't get enough of. Marsha and I would avoid the conversation and go out on the floor. We'd cull through the paperbacks, pulling the odd title, cleaning up the magazine rack after a kid had riffled it.

We worked alone together in the morning when the place was really deserted. I was on my knees counting magazines in and out. Marsha sat at the counter up front. She would read to me. Last month's magazines I was sending back were all around. I mean no one was in the store, and I would hear her read one of those short, short stories from the women's magazines. I'd lose track, counting, tune out a bit and come back on some lovers doing something then cut my palms on the paper as I slid *Scale Modeler* into its place.

"Well, what do you think will happen?" She'd stop like that, and we'd guess the ending of the story. I mean, you could guess the ending. She really loves her husband. Her kids are a joy even though they are brats. Her mother isn't going to be around much longer so she learns to be patient. They were the type of story where the baby everyone is worried about turns out to be Hitler or something. Things were always turning out. People came to realize.

I still think Marsha had a sentimental streak and liked these stories. She'd slowly page through last month's *Bride* looking at the old new dresses. I'd see her even though I was way down in the wrestling section. I'd see her bent over the two-page spread. The floor islands had little signs for the category of books. Romance SciFi. Detective Cookbook. Western Religion. Of course, she looked like she was crying — all round-shouldered, heaving sighs. I don't know.

"I don't know," I'd say. "She finds out the creep really is the one for her, that money isn't everything. I don't know." Turns out that the creep isn't a creep after all because he points out the good qualities in the man she was going to marry in the first place. He gets to be in their wedding.

We'd laugh as the things worked themselves out.

Have I given you a sense of how big this magazine rack was? It took most of the day twice a week to do a fourth of it. The copies came in bundles of ten or so apiece. More for the crosswords, less for *Atlantic*. Ten or fifteen bundles to the cardboard shipping case. Twelve or more cases. I filled most of them up again with returns. I'm not even counting the men's magazines, which were separate deliveries. I liked watching something catch on like jogging, say, sweeping through the stand, each group of magazines infecting the next — running with your dog, building your own locker room. Then there'd come new jogging magazines. Or houseplants. So even though there was the variety, it was really all the same stuff. What I'm trying to get at here is the predictability and the boredom of working in a place like Reader's World.

There's reading and there's reading, you know. And this wasn't that kind of bookstore.

So we were sort of thrown together by circumstances. She was the only living thing around. I mean the parking lot was empty most of the time.

When Marsha found something she really liked she'd read it to herself. That's how you could tell. We didn't make fun. She'd say, "Here, read this," and I'd have the queer feeling of having somebody watching when you're doing something else and I'd read the piece. This isn't to say our tastes were the same. It might have been a brief description of a place or a bit of conversation. What was I going to say, I didn't like it, when I'd have to say it looking right at her? She was sitting on the high stool with her feet up on the special-order shelf. She was a little bit older than me. "You really liked it?" she said.

That was the summer of the pubic-hair wars. That's what they called it in the business. *Penthouse* had taken out ads in the trade magazine. Saying that it was going rabbit hunting. *Playboy* had drawn a line a long time ago at breasts and behinds. Now suddenly in the packing cases were all these new magazines. The pictures were changing, the women were being turned around slowly. On the cover of one the angle had changed. You could make out an aureole behind a hand that usually hid the breast. Marsha pointed it out to me. And then she went through the lot — *Gallery, Oui, Cavalier* — and put together a kind of hierarchy that had to do with hands and mouths and hair and the number of pictures on the page, the number of pages given over to pictures.

Marsha and I looked at the women, compared this month's design to the last month's I'd just taken off the rack. The change was so slight. "Look," she said. She was serious. "Three fingers now, not two. She has pearls this time instead of flowers." It was that abstract to her. She was that removed.

The women in the pictures were all pretty enough in that way, the smooth airbrushed skin. Or the steam. "Vaseline on the lens," Marsha said. Cars and beds. I don't mean to be so objective; it was pretty amazing. It had the excitement and the caution, you know. Seeing it, so much subtlety, I pretended not to care, and I was kind of embarrassed, too, with Marsha so interested, studying the bodies. After all, she was a woman. "Put the thing away," I told her. She was unfolding one of the foldouts by the window.

"Look at that, a hand on a hip without a glove. It's so funny," she said without laughing.

What could I do but agree, go along with her calculations, her opinions? She had me on the spot. I didn't want to seem too interested. I was half-looking. I watched her study the shadows above a thigh. She turned a page and caught her breath. There were women now with and without tan lines, two women who might the next time touch each other or, beyond that, kiss. Now a clothed man, maybe, in the background instead of the car or white glider or mink. You could see which way that was going.

"Yeah, it's funny to think someone doing this, I mean, making the plans for it, winning ground, figuring it all out."

"Making this okay," she said, "or that. Getting us used to it."

So those were the wars, and I never did come up with the proper way to act. Certain lines weren't crossed, you can imagine. And those ladies who worked with us and their friends who came to visit didn't push back, didn't even notice the slight new angle to things, how it had changed. How it was a whole new world.

I remember Marsha just looking at the little boys who were climbing all over the tiers of racks, the fat flat copies of the home and garden magazines, just to see the covers. She looked, and they took off through the door, and she came back to the counter where I was counting returns. "Boys," she said, laughing.

But I remember best her reading. Her voice was bright. A stack of slick magazines fanned out across the floor. I'd given up, taken a break. She used different voices for the different characters, tried an accent or started over with another more southern, less Texan. I rolled over on my back between some canyons of books, looked up at some promotional mobile, and listened to the story about some boy and girl. I winced audibly at the dog part or the ice-cream part just to let her know I was listening.

"Do you want me to go on?" she called.

"Sure," I called back. I knew the ending. I just liked her voice and knowing that everything, and that included the rack I was working on, was neat and in place.

It was a bad location.

Like I said, the store was designed for big-volume business, and nothing was leaving the store. We just moved things in and took them off. Later they closed the store down, found other places that worked, but by then we were both gone. The pay wasn't much, but you could get free books. See, the commodity part, the legal tender of a book or magazine, is the front cover. That's the proof of purchase. That's what goes back to the publisher when you claim a refund. We got all the free stuff we wanted. Just ripped the front cover off, boom, and sent it back in with the returns. It counted. Usually they did the stripping down at the warehouse. The pulp also was destroyed there, because that's part of the deal.

I remember all of the women's magazines, a whole section by themselves. *Redbook, McCall's, Good Housekeeping, Journal.* They all had faces on the cover. There was printing on the chins or cheeks or foreheads. Huge faces. And I'm ripping these front covers off, tearing them one at a time so I can give Marsha the magazines, and the back covers with quilt ads and pictures of food and refrigerators are falling off the magazines since there is nothing to hold them on to anything anymore, and they're floating down into a pile at my feet. Then I put all these faces in a case, and they're all kind of the same — fresh, smiles. They look out, well, joyously, radiant. Happy.

I really don't know what to make of all of this. It was seeing Marsha again after all these years and thinking about all the things I've read since that summer. Good things. I was standing there in the middle of the mall with my hand on her middle, people all around. Marsha was going on, but I wasn't listening. I was looking at her face and trying to think of some lies to tell her about my own life. This is what came back to me.

CARBONATION

"The first one out is a dum-dum round," Jerry said, holding up the bullet so that we all could see. "That assumes your first target is a man. You want to knock him down." The cylinder clicked as he turned it to the next chamber. "This one is armor-piercing. It'll go through anything." He tweezed the shell between his thumb and finger. "See the point," he pointed, "it's a different metal altogether. Teflon. We use this to stop escaping vehicles. After that is a shotgun shell, or it works the same. Then, a round with an impact tip. Some use incendiary. Another flat-nosed round and then a regular round for targeting anyone that gets away. A long shot." Jerry reassembled the magnum, making sure the right chamber led into the pin. "It's what we call a scenario," he said.

Mr. Churn was in the house again because of the cars, and we could already hear him piling the cans on the front desk. Jerry came out front with us. Usually Jerry would not have been around this late or in his uniform, but because of the cars, he was staying all night. Last year someone poured a Coke on a Cord, ruining the finish, and the management had a hard time convincing the car owners to return this year.

Mr. Churn already had six or seven six-packs of Pepsi on the desk. They were made up of commemorative cans for the Auburn, Cord, Duesenberg festival.

"Hi," he said. "I made a little house." We knew he would be drunk. He asked about his wife. If she had been asking about him. We could see the way he had parked his jeep on the front lawn. "This should insure your loyalty," he said, indicating the cans. He was dressed in white to set off the tan he had obtained during a summer of sponsoring tennis tournaments. Mr. Churn was the president of RKO Bottlers. He was most of what was left of the company that had once filmed *King Kong* and *Citizen Kane*.

"We brought sound to film," he said to the clerk who was related to Tris Speaker. "In a big way." Last year with the antique cars parked for the night, Mr. Churn stumbled in joyously concluding that the Depression had returned and with it Prohibition and then handed out sixteen-ounce bottles of Pepsi like cigars.

Jerry and I were already drinking a can of this year's Pepsi as Mr. Churn finished his company's history by imitating the globe and tower trademark of RKO, twirling with his hands steepled above his head. "Tolu, tolu," he said radiating. "Surely you remember."

And then his mood changed. He told us he had yet to meet Tony Hulman, who was also staying here because of the cars. Mr. Hulman owned the Indianapolis 500, but his money came from his Coca-Cola concerns. Mr. Churn also reasoned that Mr. Hulman controlled the patent on the "hobble-skirt" bottle that had been designed in Terre Haute. "He's a great man," Mr. Churn added. Then he asked us what he should tell his wife.

We suggested that he use a meeting with Mr. Hulman as an alibi. And Mr. Churn said that he wouldn't be surprised if the old fart only drank Coca-Cola. "Besides I don't need an alkali; I need a story."

This reminded him of something else. "You know," he said, "life is only slices of life." And then he told us about the car auction and the balloon ascension his company sponsored and the picnic after the automobile parade. We were very nice and thanked him, reminding him that we slept during the day. We said that everyone seemed to have a good time here on Labor Day. "I was just recalling some antidotes for your benefit," Mr.

Churn said. He then went back out to his jeep. He hit his head on the striped top, swatted at the fringe. He drove across the lawn, swerving close to Hilter's staff car. That's when Jerry thought he better go outside and take a look around.

A little bit later, a city policeman came in looking for a guest who might be driving a red, white and blue jeep. We gave him one of the six-packs. Of course, we knew who it was. So I took the master ring and told the cop I would meet him by Mr. Churn's room. The other clerk would direct him there and see if we could find Jerry on the property. It seemed routine. Something to do with a traffic accident, I understood.

On my way back to the room, I heard the first shots. The pop. Pop. Different in degrees.

❖

Where does a boy learn poetry but in his grandpa's house? "Coffee, Mawkey! Cream, Dream! Sugar, Buger!" The magic formula for a drink handed down from generation to generation. This family business. He drank coffee right after the meal. In a big milk-colored mug, he shredded a piece of stale bread and soaked it in the white coffee for dessert.

He told me the baby's first smile is caused by gas. There are other forms of expression left to the infant — spitting up, wetting, the dirt itself. But he remembers that smile.

In the summer my brother and I would put Grandpa's Pepsi in the front lawn and wait for it to explode. Two or three at a time. Which one would go first? We watched the crowns, the bottle, the Romanesque twist of sunlight. The shoulders shrugging. The percolation of incidents. And then the whole business. The whole brown column toppling over. How could they contain so much?

We knew nothing of pressure, temperature, the standard things at sea level. Grandpa would shake out the gas sometimes. He pressed his thumb over the bottle's mouth. He put his whole arm into it. The foam would rush to fill the space, flow up the neck and layer itself into beige chiffon. He let us drink through the gas. We realized in the first panic of inhaling that air could be tasted, that it was made up of portions of different things all unseen. Those simple things. Chemistry started there with Priestly,

CARBONATION   87

Boyle, and Lavoisier generating carbon dioxide from their imagination, hoping to imitate the holy sparkling water from the spas. The first applied science. Getting to the dead syrup underneath, we learned suspension and suspense in one swig.

He drank Pepsi for his health. How the man could belch. Healthy, he thought. At night on the back porch, he sat and uttered a scale of decreasing volume or one sustained note, finished, and took another shot.

Once, he listed all the strange flavors he had tasted. Tasted in soda pop.

Almond, Asphodel, Banana, Blood Orange, Calisaya, Catawba, Celery, Checkerberry, Coffee, Cream, Kola Champagne, Lactart, Maple, Orgreat, Pistachio, Rose, Sarsaparilla, Syrup of Violets, Walnut Cream, Wintergreen. No more description than that. "Soda" itself extinct as an ingredient except as a part of the name.

The night sky was always expanding over the dying elm trees. He would whistle across the mouth of the empty bottle. The standard things. The one-note symphony. He would scrape the cork liner from the inside of the bottle cap.

Come on, come on. You're the Pepsi generation.

Come on, come on. Join the celebration.

Let him dissolve into this or that commercial. It seems all right for a minute. The things we contain. Snatches of songs, traces of extracts, elixirs, essences. Fusillade. Fizz. The redoubt. The delaying action. The skirmishes of half-life. The bubbles bursting in air.

❖

"This is our life," one of the workers said, "all of us now have to work part-time jobs and then picket just to live." Three of them were sitting up on a raised platform talking to a large crowd of students. "You know that their largest customer is this university." The drivers' strike had been going on for two years now, and this was another attempt by the union to generate a boycott of Coca-Cola on campus. "Coke is a good product. I wouldn't drive for anybody else, but look what this has done to my family."

Some of the audience, even those who might have been sympathetic to the union position, sipped from the red paper cups or used empty Coke cans as ashtrays. They listened to the familiar history of walkouts, scabs, lockouts, union-busting, arbitration, harassment, suits. The conspiracy involving the Teamsters International and Coca-Cola was mentioned. Incidents of syrup trucks crossing picket lines were substantiated. It was then revealed that the university allowed the company's trucks the use of the football stadium in the off-season as means of protection from vandalism. A university official answered that the company paid rent.

One or two of the drivers wore their pin-stripe uniforms. "How can you drink that stuff?" one of them asked. "It's poison."

"It's good," someone answered from the room, meaning, I think, to be satiric. But it might have been delivered in all honesty. And the drivers left. All that remained was to read a statement issued by the bottler, who would not come to the meeting. "In fear," he wrote, "of my life."

The strike lasted two more years. A man was shot at the football stadium.

❖

The empty can rolled back and forth on the floor of the cab. Sometimes it would stick under the front seat when we stopped and roll back out when we started up again. This was our first trip to the city, and we were sharing the cab with a man who had been on our airplane. He worked for the Pepsi-Cola Company, Purchase, New York, and had met Joan Crawford.

We expressed to him our fears about the safety of the city, and he assured us that in all of his travels he never felt more at home than when he was here in the city. He said that he traveled for his company and that it was his profession to ask for a Coke in establishments having an exclusive agreement with Pepsi-Cola. We could not contain our surprise that there actually were such people. We remarked that we had better watch what we say, and in his turn he related many interesting anecdotes in a matter-of-fact tone, including an incident in Paris, which he recounted in

French. He was present at the dedication of the first bottling plant in the Soviet Union, where, he also told us, there is a longer line for a Coke than there is to view Lenin. "But most of my work centers around local fountains such as those." He pointed to the passing storefronts. "You would be surprised how many times I am not corrected. My company is willing to spend millions of dollars to prevent our name from slipping into lowercase." He laughed.

He suggested that we visit the Coca-Cola Museum in Atlanta, which contains the most extensive collection of proprietary bottles in the world. He traced the history of the carbonated-drink industry in America.

"I like to cite Justice Holmes." And he did. We wrote it down. It was in the case of the Coca-Cola Company versus Koke Company of America in the U.S. Supreme Court, 1921. "I find in it legitimacy," Justice Holmes, holding for Coke, wrote: "The name now characterizes a beverage to be had at almost any soda fountain. It means a single thing coming from a single source and well-known to the community. It hardly would be too much to say that the drink characterizes the name as much as the name the drink." "Italics mine," he said, but we noticed none. "You can see the ramifications?" We nodded. What could we say?

In the city proper the only things our friend would say came after we passed the Candler Building with all its billboards. "Pop contributed greatly to education. Both Tufts and Emory were founded on such fortunes. Both with medical schools demonstrating the close connection of the industry with public health. The industry's contribution to advertising is unquestioned."

When we reached our hotel he leaned over and asked, "At least, you found these things interesting?"

"At the very least," we answered. I tell you it was something to run into a man who you never thought existed and have a chance to talk to him. He *was* very interesting to say the least and a wonderful introduction to what we thought was an unfriendly city.

What I think is funny is that later, when we were robbed, all that crossed my mind was that the revolver was a cola color.

❖

SAFETY PATROL

One note. It begins with that and usually, out of habit, leads to another culminating in a crowd of people. Places. Things. A party. Party music. Voices over. Or. A man alone, unconscious of any consensus doing the things he wants to do. That kind of man. By his very indifference he is chosen to lead us to drink. Culminating in consensus. The campaign. Hi-C.

He is aware, as an artist, that there are certain internal forms that one invokes to give the world some sense. This one note, the jingle writer thinks, is the thing that satisfies best. The real thing. The Coca-Cola Company of Atlanta, his client, has just recently purchased, lock, stock, and barrel, Hi-C.

There is nowhere else to begin but on that note. It is natural. This private opening into composition.

And what follows naturally is the sixty seconds. The sixty-second notes or nearest fraction thereof. The sixty other things that convince us consuming is communal. Even when alone. The bottle. The can. The glass. Compare. Contents. Condensation always. In the air gas infused (that is the technical term) in liquid. States confused. The Calvin scale. It is a song everyone can sing. The beat of the swallow. The taste that beats the others cold. Associations. The fizz itself. The guttural pour. The splash. The crack of ice. The bubbles rising again. The name itself. Let it speak. Pop.

Empty whole notes rising to the occasion. Every good boy deserves fudge. Favors. Does fine. This satisfies. Does everyone follow. Scene. A midwestern festival. Balloons rising. Interest in old machinery. Thresher? Combine. A way to introduce former slogans. The Pause that refreshes. Longings. 1929. Candler dies. The serving trays. People laughing at how they used to look. Scene. Returning empty bottles. Boys. A wagon. A dog keeps time. Balloons rising. Satisfaction. Money back. Earned refreshment tastes better. Scene. Workers themselves happily working. Perspiration. Condensation. Much better. Skeleton of high rise. Balloons rising. Hard hats. Bottle caps. Eye-catching sandwiches. Scene. A ride in the park. Handsome hansoms. Central Park singing. The buildings rising. Balloons rising. Someone tips his hat. Bottle cap. Dissolve. Scene. A boy and his grandfather. Someone old at least. A generation. Two generations. Chord change. Can there be a sprinkler? A falling star? Balloons rising.

Someone winks. The child cries. Grandpa burps. No. Scene. A man in a room at the piano. Wood floor. Sheet music. The bottle. The people. Where are the people? Balloons rising? He has finished the song they are singing. He is writing the song they have been singing. He is writing the song they have already sung. He is improvising. He is fooling around. Chopsticks. Someone sends out for Chinese. Pizza. Hamburgers. Eye-catching sandwiches. Someone burps. No.

He is stuck.

He remembers something that he read once. Written before his time.

> Pepsi-Cola hits the spot.
> Twelve full ounces, that's a lot.

That's better. Pause. Rest. Swig of Coke. Wash of Coke. Splash of Coke. Inspiration. Dead. The empty bottle. The thing itself. Drawing to it. Meaning. The Universe. Space. That's catchy, but it's not filling. All the good things. What do you want? To be done. It is, after all, a soft drink. Perhaps a melody that lingers. An aftertaste? Is that desired? The money. The sound of it.

> Coke adds life.
> Everybody wants a little life.
> Coke adds life.
> Everybody wants.

Let the bottle say the rest. The goods speak for themselves. Voices over. Balloons rising. Comic afterthoughts.

A man at a window looking out across the roofs. The measure of an automatic clip emptying. The answering rounds closer. Single shots. Aimed.

❖

What did we need money for? We would spend at least part of every summer day at the drugstore. The chocolate candy would have been replaced by the less perishable hard rock candy, Life Savers, Dum-Dum suckers, Pez in cartoon shooters, or those paraffin disguises — huge red lips with teeth. There were sculptured wax bottles filled with colored sugar water. To get at it you had to bite right through the neck. Sometimes we would just get a flavored Coke or phosphate in Dixie cups with the hearts or the larger cup that said HUM DINGER. Or snow cones, anything that would change the color of our mouths.

We got our money by returning empties. We would even take the one that Grandma used to dampen clothes with when she ironed. We took out the special spigot she used and spirited away the pop bottle. "Rats in the pantry," she would call after us. We would leave her bubble gum from the baseball cards as an offering, knowing all the time that we would not only have the money from the deposit but the soda from the new bottle she would have to buy.

We would find empty bottles everywhere. Take the one Grandpa used when he weeded the lawn, still some killer in the bottom. We loaded up our wagons with mixed cartons of Coca-Cola and Pepsi, 7-Up, Hires, Nehi, Nesbitt's, Dr. Pepper, RC and Orange Crush. We went to the supermarket because they would take every brand.

One day we found a dead man in the bottle bin at the supermarket. One of the old men who worked there in semiretirement. He was just draped over the side of the cart. His hands hung down and open by the empty bottles. His face was blue. It looked like he was just arranging something at the bottom of the bin. We were close enough to tell. My brother peered over the edge of the bin. I unloaded the wagons. All the other people in the store went on working, ringing out sales, giving stamps, sacking. He wouldn't come to life. So we just left. Left the bottles. We saw him through the windows, his back humped over. On the way home we kept looking over our shoulders. Surrounded by all those signs of death, all I remember by brother saying was, "Where is the blood?"

MARCH OF DIMES

As we walk to the next house, I tell my son to hold up. The back of his coat is folded up from sitting. It looks like a little tail. Beneath his coat I can see where his white shirt has come untucked. It glows raggedly against the seat of his pants. "Stand up straight." He does. He's all bundled up. His arms, in the quilted sleeves, seem to float at his sides. His hood is up and clinched around his face glowing like his shirt. His face is pale and smooth in the light so you want to touch it. In the corners of his mouth, I know there are those little smile lines made by the Dixiecup of grape Kool-Aid at the last house. "Wipe your mouth." I put the envelope and clipboard down on the ground by his feet as I kneel in front of him. Reaching around behind, I work my thumbs into the back of his elastic breeches, tucking as I go, then a quick zip around each half of the trunk of his body. "There." I yank down at the hem of his coat with both hands. The hood tightens around his head. He hops a little after each yank as if he were a compressed spring released. His arms seem only connected to his body by the sleeves of his coat. I tuck some hair back up inside his hood and touch his face.

I pick up my things and stand up. We start walking again to

the next house. There are not many lights on in the houses on the block. All downstairs. The blue light of TVs or fish tanks. Cars pass rarely on the cross street up ahead. I can hear the corduroy switch of his trousers as he walks next to me. My husband thinks I bring our son along as some type of illustration. An example of good health. A general reminder.

The moon is full and in the trees. I exaggerate the swinging of my arms so that I can feel the coins slide back and forth in the envelope. Some stick in the tight corners. I can feel the face of one through the paper. My writing on the envelope is distorted by the coins beneath the surface. I can rub the pencil back and forth using the long part of the lead and make the face appear.

The next house has an enclosed porch. I can hear the slap of his oxfords on the cement walk. The jingle of coins. I never know what to do when I come to a house with an enclosed porch. I've done both. I've stood outside the porch door and pounded, hoping they would hear me through both doors. I've pounded so hard the screens rattled. And I have crept into the porch with its shadows of summer furniture or old sofas, the bikes and rag rugs and tapped on the inside door. When I first hear the conversation stop or when they are just silent differently, I know they have heard something. And then I tap again until I feel their footsteps coming to the door through my own feet. I try to be but never am ready for when the door swings open and I am discovered in the half-light. I find myself in some half-room of their house. "The Mother's March," I say.

This house has a doorbell outside, and my son wants to ring it. The doorbell is lit, a little dime-sized moon. I lift him up, and when he pokes the button, the light goes off. In the house, we hear the bells, three of them, the silence and then someone coming. The doorbell light pulses on again after he lets up. "Pick up the paper so you can hand it to the lady." The porch light comes on. The inside door opens, then the storm, and then a Mrs. James Payne pads across the porch. We can see her through the porch storm. She still can't see us because the glass of the storm reflects the light inside back toward her. The overlapping louvers on the storm slowly open as she cranks them. We are watching her be cautious.

"Who's there?"

"The Mother's March," I say.

"Come in. Come in."

In a way, my husband is right. My son sits in another chair, holding a glass of something else which he supports with both hands. He never takes the glass from his lips. Tips it a bit more now and then. He swings his legs, looks around the room over the rim of the glass. The woman whose house we are in is reading through the brochures, tsking over the children with braces. Those children have brilliant smiles. She steals a glance at my son, who has focused his attention on an array of porcelain thimbles next to him on the table. I know it is a matter of touching and not touching. The newspaper, still folded, is beneath his swinging feet. She is going to get her purse, more soda.

I am unspooling that endless twine from the two red paper buttons on the back of the envelope. I have been opening and closing the envelope flap all night, and each time I do, I wrap the string around in a different pattern. This is my first winter collecting for the March of Dimes. I am halfway through the names and addresses. My map is spotty with "at homes" and "aways." Many people still talk about Roosevelt. It is an older neighborhood. Few children. These women make me lonely with their grown-up children framed on the coffee table. My husband is only half-right. "Don't touch," I tell my son.

I wish I was able to repeat the things my son says in the way he says them. But I can never find the words. Precious, you know, cute. But any time mothers repeat the words of their children, it never sounds quite right. It is always the parent talking. Still, children mimic their mothers and dads, I know. That is what makes them cute. Or maybe it is both ways. In any case, my husband is right about some of the uses for children. My son keeps me company between the houses even though we are silent. "Let Mommy talk," I say to him as he pushes past the neighbor holding the screen door open. He finds his own chair. Let Mommy talk, indeed. See how the words change when we use them.

❖

SAFETY PATROL

It is eight o'clock and, even though we are not tired, we turn for home. The pamphlet that comes with the soliciting kit suggests this. We are walking again. He hasn't asked me to carry him. In his neighborhood the streetlights are the old candy-cane type, globes suspended over the street, the top hemisphere blackened still from the war. The vaccine's already found. My baby is already born and walking. Perfect. All his toes and fingers. He started talking early. Perfect. I am collecting for this, for him. For the time when I didn't know yet. It should be more than that. I tell him about polio and the summers his grandmother wouldn't let me swim. How, when I was his age, I was never allowed to be cold. I think quickly to ask if he is cold now. He isn't. As he switches and slaps in the dark next to me, he chants *polio* again and again. It will be his word for awhile. He'll repeat it when he is thinking to himself, as he did with the word *sum*.

❖

When we get home, my husband is mixing blood in the kitchen. He is a safety director for the local phone company. He investigates accidents when company cars or trucks are involved and writes up the police reports in the passive voice. On the dashboards of the mangled vehicles, he has already stuck decals about backing and looking both ways. He lectures to linemen and switchmen on artificial respiration, electrocution and shock. The blood is for some first-aid simulation he does. In the trunk of his car, there is a kit filled with realistic rubber casts of burns and fractures. He fills a special bladder with the blood. He wears it strapped beneath a beat-up shirt. Hoses are taped to his body and along his arm. He squeezes a rubber ball from an atomizer to pump the blood to a severed artery at his wrist or knee. I have seen him die a couple of times when rookie framemen applied the wrong kind of direct pressure or put the tourniquet below the wound. In times of emergencies people just yell, "Don't move him. Don't move him." He bleeds to death.

He is sprinkling an old shirt with blood, using the 7-Up bottle and the plastic spray spigot I use to dampen clothes I'm ironing.

"How did it go?" he asks, gore to the elbows.

Odd. He is the type who gets queazy at things like that, leaves the room when I do my nails because of the ether smell, turns off hospital shows. He lets me dig for splinters, pop blisters. At the doctor's, he faints when his reflexes are tested. He stumbles out of the office, sicker than ever before. As I fill the prescription he sits on the little couch with his head between his knees. He cannot stomach listening to people tell of their operations or having their hands closed in doors or even losing toenails. At night in bed, he will toss for hours, cannot sleep if he hears his own heart beating in his ears.

"I was the one they watched in driver's education class when they showed the films," he told me. I think it is the words that bother him most of all. *Laceration* for *cut*. The slow accumulation of the sounds.

His hands are red and he squeezes me on both my arms with the inside of his.

"What did the little one bring in?" he asks.

"He's counting it now," I tell him. "We're halfway through. We'll go out again tomorrow."

He turns back to an old bowling shirt, *Tony* on the pocket. "Like an organ grinder's monkey."

I'm used to it. You get used to it.

I tip my finger in his blood, touch him lightly on the forehead, square on his football scar.

"Hey," he says.

He can't do anything about it now. His arms raised at the elbows. He looks like a surgeon with gloves on.

Our son has been counting and stacking the coins. He gets to keep all the pennies. He stores his pennies in an Old Grandad bottle his father says he came out of.

"How did we do?" I ask him.

I think he thinks it is somewhat like Hallowe'en but grown-up without the candy, and he seems to arrange the coins like candy about him except there is less of it. He freezes most of the candy bars he gets for trick-or-treating and eats the chocolate coins wrapped in gold tin foil right way. He tells me $27.20. He has thirty-six pennies for his bottle.

"Aren't you tired?" I ask him. I'm tired. Without my glasses, the stacks of coins seem to be sprouting from the carpet, silver stocks. It has been a sheepish March. Nice during the day, chilly at night. It is supposed to snow a bit tomorrow. He has gone to get the plastic sherbet tub we keep the money in. I can hear him making faces at his father's mess and then giggles and splashes. Of course, he will come out and try and touch me with sticky hands. I am already halfway up the stairs when he reaches the bottom, hands out and clawing. Maybe when he grows up he won't be like his father that way. Used to it. He took his boosters okay as long as I was there, and he squirted the neighborhood kids with the syringe the doctor gave him. His father could not look at the Tb test on his son's arm and made him wear long sleeves in early fall. Maybe blood will never be real to him.

"Come here, you monster," I drag him by the elbows into the bathroom and wash it off into the sink. I strip him to his underwear. He is brushing his teeth, back and forth, not up and down. He stands there, using every muscle he has in his body to keep his head perfectly still. His hand saws away. I notice the button of his vaccine. It seems to be the head of the pin holding his arm on. Still, in relief, pinker than his skin, still round. The center of a black-eyed Susan. I remember when the scab fell off. We were so careful not to touch it before it did.

He pees for a long time because of all the soda and Kool-Aid. As he does he whispers something to himself.

Tucked in bed, he tells me the name of each face on the coins, wonders why Lincoln is facing the wrong way and Roosevelt's neck is too short. He says he likes going into other people's houses and can't wait until we go out again tomorrow.

"I couldn't do it without you. You're a good helper," and catch myself from going on in this way, talking like other mothers talk. *Mommy's little helper.* Why do I want to talk this way? "I'll see you tomorrow. We'll go out again."

Downstairs, my husband is done with blood and has washed his hands. He has forgotten where I've touched him. I can still see the edges of the print beneath the fringe of hair. He is at work now, diagramming accidents on graph paper with colored pencils. Sometimes he scoots tokens from board games across the grid to give him a better feel for what happened. He goes over and over the accident, concludes, finally, it was following distance or overdriving headlights.

"You have to get the big picture," he tells me. "Drive defensively. Leave yourself an out." When he drives in his own car, he mutters at other drivers, becomes furious at old women in crosswalks. I watch him from my side of the seat as he thinks about his job. I say nothing, find my right foot pressing the floor, try not to move so he won't say, "What you jumping for? We're okay. We're okay."

My son's miscounted. $28.35. I throw in my husband's loose change. I fill in the reports. The poster child is thanking me. It looks as if she has climbed the long ladder of printed lines that scale the left margin of the page — staff, directors, honorary chairmen — to her perch in the upper corner. Roosevelt looks at her across the top of the page, through *Liberty,* chin up, hair cut, without his glasses too. The date on the coin is the year of my son's birth. I dump the coins in the sherbet tub. They arrange themselves the way coins do, scalloped or scaled, deepening in sound as they deepen in the tub. The poster child has braces and metal crutches, the tops of which are strapped to her forearm. She leans out from the paper. What would she say? I draw a cartoon coming from her mouth. *Polio. Polio.* Not, *Won't you help me? Sometimes, I am weary of courage.* But a child would not talk that way.

My husband heads by me, up to bed. He runs his fingers across my shoulder as he goes.

"I'll be right there." I plan my route for the next night, sharing the streets with paperboys collecting, Girl Scouts and cookies, cars driving down the side streets with their brights on. People can't guess who is at their doors.

I look in at my son's room. I wait in the doorway until my eyes adjust. The moon is high now and in the window. The linoleum has an egg-speckled pattern on dark brown. We ironed it to the floor ourselves. I can only hear one-half of his breathing — breathing in — so it sounds as if he is making a higher-pitched sound each time he does. I see his head on its side, a shoulder and arm emerging. He looks like my coin rubbings, soft and out of focus. The light picks up something on his finger. A Band-Aid? I go over and kneel down beside him. It is a porcelain thimble. Bathroom-sink white. There is a bundle of violets painted on the collar. The little pockmarks of the tip have their own shadows, each a phase of the moon in the moonlight.

I ease it off his finger and put it on mine. I don't like the way it feels. Touching but not touching. The way being touched someplace is never the same as touching the place yourself. But touching the head of the thimble itself, its curve, its roughness is pleasing. It almost feels grainy as if instead of scoops there are spheres dotting the tip. What would it feel like if I didn't know what it was? Its opposite? The ridges of a finger?

I slip it back on one of his fingers. A different finger. Will that make him think in the morning? Wonder how it got there. His fingers walk. His thimble goes from house to house.

I am about to wake my husband and tell him, but I don't. I don't know what I would tell him. We all have our own lives in this house, and these two do not meet here. He is dreaming of game-board tokens making wrong turns, graphs of fatalities. Accidents. He wasn't drunk that night. I wasn't drunk that night. The only difference was our son, no accident. He took.

My husband's back is toward me. He has slept through the noise of his heart. I can barely see his vaccine, dimpled in his arm. A print. A daylight moon. I touch it as I fit in behind him.

About the time I became pregnant, we took the oral vaccine in the national program at the junior high. It was a Sunday, and the halls were filled with well-dressed neighbors lined against the lockers leading toward the girls' gym. We would take a couple of steps then stop. He would fiddle with the nearest locker. I read the brochures, sometimes reading parts aloud to him. The hall was close and warm. The ceiling was low. "No shots," I told him, "just sugar."

Down the ramp and into the gym. We stopped to sign our names. The hallway opened up to two stories. The sun slanted through windows with metal screens to protect them from the balls. It gave the sunshine in the gym a mottled look. The floor was linoleum. The boys' gym was wood. A doctor and several nurses handed out the sugar cubes. The way they were bricked together made them look like a junior high school project of the walls of Troy.

"Do you have some water?" my husband asked.

"You don't swallow it. Suck on it. It's just sugar."

"I'd like some water," he said.

"In the hall. Outside."

The sugar tasted sweet, of course. My teeth rang when I bit into the cube. My mouth was sticky. My husband could barely get his down. We were out by the line again, by a drinking fountain much too low for him.

"Oh, c'mon. It's not that bad," I said.

"Yeah?" he said. "I just don't like sweet things. Okay? Okay?"

People in line looked at us. Crouching, he drank with his eyes open, his face as white as the fountain. We sat on the steps outside for a long while.

Sweet thing, I am used to it. I have lived with it long enough.

❖

There is only a powder of snow. We are marching through the neighborhood. It seems that everyone is expecting something. The porch lights are all on. This is what charity should be. Door-to-door. Face-to-face. I do not like the loose change in checkout lanes with the plastic hourglasses or the cardboard sheets with penny-loafer slots and fading football players. I'm a mother, too, not a movie star. This is my son.

The moon is full again but starting to melt. Its light looks good on the snow, white with streaks of yellow from the porches. He reads the house numbers and tries to guess the next one. Our envelope is heavy. The coins knife back and forth.

At a corner, before we cross, I ask him about the thimble. I smile to myself as his eyes widen. I know they widen even though I cannot see them. What can he say? Has he even been able to explain it to himself? He says nothing, repeats something to himself. I suggest we return it to the lady, and he agrees. Tomorrow. Yes, tomorrow. He needs it one more night. He can show it to me, now, himself.

On the bank of our yard, the one my husband hates to mow in the summer, we make very poor snow angels. The money jingles as I make the wings. There isn't enough snow here. We lie back down. The bank is steep. We are not far from standing, more like leaning backward. We blow our breath away into the night. I tell him the moon is dime-sized, no bigger. And he doesn't believe me. It is hanging there at least half-dollar size. It is the moon, after all. I sit up and unravel the flap of my envelope, reach in and feel for a dime. I find one. I tell him to hold it at arm's length and close one eye. "Put it over the moon." And he does.

Tomorrow, we will go out again, collecting.

X-RAY

Here, when he opened the door, the children began performing tricks, little things with their hands and fingers he never understood or couldn't see in the folds of the sheets. They struck poses, mumbled songs, turned flashlights off and on, shining the light up through the plastic masks. They blurted out riddles, *Why did the moron throw a clock out the window?* When he answered, they yelled. *No,* he wasn't supposed to answer. It was their trick. The bags of candy were piled like rocks in the corner of his porch. One tall girl did flips out in the yard, out into the darkness. "Look," he said, "you don't need to do this. You don't need. That's not what a trick is."

He looked down at them. They were panting, trying to see.

"Look," he said, "it means the other trick. Something bad if I don't give you a treat, you see? Something like that. Like soap. It's a threat. I'm supposed to be scared of you. The way you look. You're scarey."

He was aware of adults waiting off on the sidewalk, the air leaving his house. The tall girl in the back went up on her toes.

"Here," he said. "Here and here you go." And they thanked him.

His father could blow bubbles with his spit. He remembered watching his father. The mouth was closed but the lips working, the throat moving, inhaling air through his nose. And when he rounded his lips, he had very thin lips and the lips were wet, the tip of his tongue came out, just the tip, for a second and then the clear bubble, not like soap, heavy and clear, the size of a BB. Two or three at a time. It was the most delicate thing he remembered his father doing, the way he lifted his chin.

He could never do that. He tried. He could scoop a bubble up from behind his lower teeth and rest it on his tongue. He could do that right now. But when he moved his mouth, puckered his lips, the bubble broke. He heard it break through the bones in his head. It sounded like his jaw cracking hollow, wooden.

When he was a boy, he always said he was double-jointed when he needed to say something like that. His friends were sitting around him belching and farting.

"Watch this," he said and dug the heel of his hand into the ground next to where he was sitting. He screwed his arm back and forth from the wrist. It wasn't much of a trick. Everyone who saw it tried it, but no one could twist the forearm, the elbow like he did without picking up a hand. He didn't know why.

He didn't know about this either. These tricks. It was more a performance, role memory. Or something made up on the spot. Everything was quickly rehearsed, even the tumbling, nothing emanating from the boredom of the long afternoons here.

There was a cicada hatch this summer. Not a big one, but the sawing was noticeable at dusk when he walked the empty streets. And downtown he saw several stunned adult insects, their wings stretched out, on the ledges of the big store windows they had hit. He had collected a large mayonnaise jar — he had emptied the mayonnaise into the bathtub — full of the golden shells he picked off the tree trunks and brick houses, the concrete light poles, the snow fences.

He liked the angle of the front legs. Now there was an insect. The broad forehead between the polished eyes, the stubby body and filmy wings. The scale, too, was right. There was a real bit of terror, a heft, when one flew by slowly, cigar butts. Dangerous. Not like the insect-sized insects — flies, bees, gnats.

No one else seemed to be gathering the shells. And now that he thought about it, the children had surprised him again. He almost worked up enough courage to invite in the next group knocking at his door and show them the jar of shells, the perfect slit down the backs. And, maybe, give some away in the light of his house, in the bags of candy. What would the parents say then? *Do you remember? Do you remember who gave you this?*

Answering the door again, he realized that he'd been here long enough now to have seen some of these children in their mother's wombs. This little one wearing a mask, the shell of a princess, her mother might have said, *It's only sound, you say.* They stared as the Polaroid developed. The thing took its shape in light, tracing a contour map, a wash on dark wax scraped with a pin. So this is how it turned out he thought to say. The princess was choking on a nursery rhyme that had to do with gardens, and the mother had asked him if everything is there where it's supposed to be.

Yes, that's the head there. There are the eyes. *It's amazing,* she said, *amazing. Can I keep this?*

By now he'd seen hundreds of the unborn children and now here they were at his door doing tricks, snapping their fingers, no longer frightening at all.

He washed his hands after handling the shells and watched television while he waited for the door to knock again. He ranged over the remote panel, his finger like a chess knight. Later, he would go to the clinic to check the candy.

❖

As a boy, he had set a bag of dog crap on fire. He rang the doorbell and ran off the porch and around the house to the back. He could hear someone in front stomping out the flames, cursing, yelling. He was at the back door ringing the doorbell there until he heard the front door slam. Then he took off through the backyard bushes, down the cinder alley. He pictured a man tramping through the house, racing to the back door, mad, unthinking, shoes all caked, ruined. And his own heart was pounding as he ran by the open garages and ashcans. Dogs barked everywhere. He thought of it again and realized that what he saw as he ran was the inside of his own family home, the living room and the furniture, since he didn't know, couldn't imagine what the inside

SAFETY PATROL

of his victim's home was like. He saw this stranger stumbling and raging through his kitchen as he ran toward his house. It was thrilling, an intruder there and a smelly fire on a porch someplace behind him.

When had the cicada stopped singing? The bugs in the halo of the street lamp, when had they gone? Now only the hum of the excited, inert gases. And the year of the hatching — eleven, thirteen, seventeen — why were they prime numbers? An X-ray of an insect would look like the insect. If we carried our bones outside, he'd be out of a job.

He could walk to the clinic from his house, and he did. When cars sped by, he heard syllables over the snatch of radio music. It always sounded as if they were yelling at him. It always surprised him. He thought of things to yell back only after the car was long gone. He wished them accidents, wished to see them later, crumbled on his table, through the lead-lined window.

Now, as he walked through town, there were still children in the shadows, their shapes distorted by their costumes. Something round huddled near a bicycle, working the combination lock. Some cubes jumped the borders between yards hurrying to the next house before the curfew and the porch lights going out. Sneakers slapped once, twice on the cement walks then were swallowed by the lawns. The dark heads, the candy bags, swung by the hair. He heard around him the little songs, the tails of sentences rising to questions, small bursts of applause, choruses of *thank yous.*

Children charged around him, the masks pushed up like ancient Greek helmets. Sucker sticks poked out of mouths. The children ran to the next house. The three hours almost gone. From far behind him, the voice. *What do you say?* And they shrieked, *Excuse me.*

Be careful, the voice came up through its murmuring. He didn't look around. *Be careful. Don't run with those things in your mouth.* A hiss, a scuff on the walk.

He had heard of an exhibit at a museum in the capital. It was a collection of objects people had swallowed, inhaled, and then had been removed and donated to the state. Class trips always stopped there, outside a field of yellow buses. The doctors he worked with told him about it. Pennies, paper clips, nails, tacks, keys, rings, all kinds of pins — bobby, hat, safety — marbles, thimbles, bullets. He had found some of those same things in people, the dark-edged shapes in the white clouds of flesh and the ropey smoke of bone. Nuts and bolts. He could count the threads. Read the time on the watch, see the guts behind the face, the teeth working. He saw the white faces of the schoolchildren on tour as they peered into the glass cases. These things were inside of people. Metal parts. They caught their breath. They swallowed without chewing. He had seen patients trying to see through their own skins. Saw them try not to. There is an outside and an inside.

He felt as if he had just shown up here in this town, appeared out of the air. The welcome wagon had given him coupons redeemable for things that could be dangerous — rulers with metal edges, cake cutters, tiny measuring spoons. The houses of the town started where the fields of corn left off. The highway became a street. The town grew by parking lots and blocks of houses. The windows of the houses were blue with televisions; the porch lights were out. As he went by each house, he saw, inside, parts of bodies. In the windows were eclipsed heads, feet on tables. There was a wedge of shoulder, a leg flashing. He saw shadows on shades and curtains rustled. And once again, he imagined only the house he grew up in and these strangers moving around inside.

He made his way through the big crowd at the clinic up to the door. He recognized a few of the doctors with their children, the faces of people who worked downtown in stores and waited tables. All of the women looked familiar. Their children faced him, too, wormed up against their mothers' thighs. The children wore satiny clothes, smooth as if from rubbing. They clutched at the arms draped over their shoulders, pressed back. *Don't be shy. He's not going to hurt you.*

"Now folks," he said, "it'll take a bit to set up the machine." And he fumbled with his keys. A baby was crying. He could hear the paper contents of the paper bags as they were shook. The dry paper. A hand being smacked. The fluoroscope was inside the door. He took off his jacket and turned on the power.

"Folks," he said, "I've got to let the machine warm up a bit." There were cartoon characters and character types. Animals and plants. All the professions, religions, crafts. Ghosts, crooks, skeletons. Skeletons.

"How do you want to do this now? I guess you could just line up here." People moved a bit, formed lines. "I should tell you that the radiation won't harm the candy or fruit. The . . ." he couldn't think of the word, "rays go right through the . . . and then it depends on the density of the things it goes through and the different thicknesses. The rays then hit the screen and excite things in the screen. Like your television and it lights up. That's what I'll see. Some things will be darker than others." They were all listening, turned his way. There was a vague sort of order.

"As I said, this procedure won't harm the contents of the wrapper. We'll just see if anyone has, you know. It's faster."

The machine was old and boxy. The door of the clinic wouldn't stay open. It was only recently that he understood that the stars moved at night. To watch time fly.

"And I liked all of the tricks this year. Didn't you?"

There was scattered applause and some children cheered. A girl shook her hands together over her head like a champion.

"Where I come from we didn't do tricks like those. Nice ones. We did other tricks. They weren't very good. The words we said, we meant something different. It was the other way around." He thought then he should be quiet. "Just a few more minutes." He looked out at the crowd. Parents talked to one another again. Children were falling asleep at their feet. He looked down.

He ordered the X-ray gogs from the back of the comic book. The rubber frames had lenses of paper printed with black and white whirlpools. A hole had been cut in the eye of the storm. There, there were transparent red pieces of plastic and sandwiched inside was something that looked like a fish skeleton but turned out to be, when he tore the whole thing apart, a feather.

If you held your hand up to the light and looked through the filters, you did see something — an aura around your hand, a crazy double image. It might be bones. The instructions said to convince your friends by letting them look at their own hands. And then you were supposed to look at a pretty girl slowly, up and down, while making appreciative sounds. You'll cause a riot, it said on the package. Everyone will want to look. He just saw the red girl, the deeper shadow. He had been afraid he would be able to see her bones, afraid that his vision would go through her clothes right through her skin. Not very pretty at all.

And the pregnant women sat on this table. Their bellies splitting open their clothes, the skin almost polished clear. "It's only sound," he said. "You won't even hear it. It's harmless, harmless."

The candy disappeared behind the screen. Sometimes the metal foil would show up, the sticks without the taffy. There, the stem and wilted leaf of an apple. Its seeds scattered on the table. There, the hook of a cashew.

He thought of each piece of candy as a house he wanted to see into. He wanted to find some afterimage left over, a floor plan or blueprint from being in its bowl by the door as if each square of the chocolate bar was a photographic plate. He wanted to know how furniture was arranged, where the light switches were, how people talked to each other when they were alone.

The children took off their costumes while they watched him. "Where did it go?"

"It's still there," he told them. He watched the screen. Mothers look relieved and thanked him. And they left dragging their children, who were thanking him and doing tricks and eating the clean candy, behind them.

Later he did find a blade from a cheap pencil sharpener embedded in an orange marshmallow peanut.

"Here's something," he said.

The child cried after not remembering which house it came from. The mother called back at him over her shoulder while pulling the child away. "It's your fault. You brought this on. No one would have dared do this. But they knew the stuff would be checked. They knew it would be X-rayed. They knew you would find it."

THE SAFETY PATROL

If you look on page 253 of the New College Edition of *The American Heritage Dictionary,* there, in the right margin toward the bottom of the page, you will find an aerial photograph of a cloverleaf interchange at Fort Wayne, Indiana.

Of the six cloverleaf interchanges in Fort Wayne, I am reasonably sure I know which one this is. It is not my favorite. That one is down the road. There, there was a small country cemetery right where the new interstate was going to go. I was on the citizens' committee that saved the place. You can still see it buried beneath the loops and ramps as they detour, twisted out of the way like a spring sprung. On some Sundays, I drive out there, drive around the place, entering and exiting. The interchange spreads for miles. I catch glimpses of the headstones — they're old, from before the Civil War — the patch of prairie grass and wild flowers, the picket fence. It is in the middle of the storm of concrete and cars. Saved. But there is no way to drive to it. All access limited, the site undisturbed. Like clouds the shadows of trucks sail over the plots, change the color of the stones.

The cloverleaf pictured in the dictionary is a perfect specimen. There has been no finagling with the curving lobes of the ramp as they coil from one dual lane to the other. If you look closely you can see snow in the ditch defining the mathematical berms, shading the grade, giving it depth and perspective. A beautiful picture, one the children are proud of.

When we do dictionary drills I include the word *cloverleaf* as a kind of Crackerjack prize for the students. They cut into the big book as I've taught them, into the first third. Some feel comfortable using the finger tabs scooped out along the edge. They turn chunks of pages, getting close, getting to *C*. They peel each page back, then read the index words *close call* and *clown,* saying the alphabet for each letter. And then, one by one, they arrive at the right page. Fingers go up and down columns. One or two gasp, then giggle. They point and whisper. They say things like "wow." They can't wait to tell me what they've found.

The cloverleaf is there with pictures of a clothes tree, a clown licking an ice-cream cone, a clover — the plant and its buds — the cloister of San Marco in Florence, Italy, an earthworm with a clitellum, and the clipper ship *Lightning*. The pictures seem to make the words they represent more important.

❖

The lights on the television and radio towers are always on even during the day, when you can barely see the flush of the red lights. The newer towers have bright strobing lights, too. You see sharp simultaneous explosions all along the edges. There are revolving lights at the very tip. Guy wires angle down so taut as to vibrate the heavy air around the towers. There are a dozen at least now, and more going up. The neighborhood is zoned for towers.

I like to play games while I look at the towers. Which one is taller? Which is furthest away? Coming up State Street on my way to teach, I watch the towers as I drive. They are solid lines, the lights slowly coming into sychronization. I am waiting for a red light, watching over the cars ahead of me down the road. Each tower is beating its own red pulse. Two or three pulse together a time or two. Then they drift apart, align with other tower lights. I know if I watch long enough, if I am lucky enough and happen to glance at the right time, I'll see all the lights on all the towers switch on and off at the very same moment.

SAFETY PATROL

The closer I get to the towers, the lacier they become. The lattice is like a kid's picture of lightning shooting down the sides. I've been to the root of some of the towers, and they are balanced at a single point on a concrete slab. There the metal flares out in an inverted pyramid, then up slightly, tapered really, but coming together anyway past the red twirling light at the top of the lone antenna pointing to a distant vanishing point.

The closer I get to the towers the more air they become. They disappear. The red and white curtain of color where they are painted in intervals hangs in the air. The lights are nearly invisible in the sun. At that certain distance, when they disappear, it is like the red line of mercury in a thermometer held slightly off-center.

I used to worry about the houses that have been built beneath the towers. They are starter homes, small, shaped like Monopoly houses, the colors of game tokens, glossy blues and reds and greens and yellows, with a trim a shade darker but the same color. The trees are puny and new, fast-growing ginkos and Lombardy poplars quaking in the breeze and spraying up like the towers way above them. The houses are scattered and crowded into cul-de-sacs and terraces like an island village. The addition is called Tower Heights. The guy wires from the towers anchor in backyards in deadeyes and turn buckles the sizes of automobiles. They are fenced off and landscaped with climbing flowers. The lines of one tower can slip beneath the lines of another, over still another, so the houses and yards are sewn up in a kind of net of cables arriving from the sky.

My students say the towers groan sometimes in storms. The wires twang. They tell me they like to lie looking up at the clouds sailing above the towers. The towers move against the clouds. They sway and topple. On a clear day, the shadows cast by the towers sweep over the houses in single file. My students take to geometry, all the lines and angles, acute, right, obtuse, the triangles, the compass point of the towers, the parallel lines. When I pull the blinds up on the window of my classroom, there, off in the distance, are the towers and wires. The roofs of their houses are just visible, a freehand line drawn beneath the proof.

❖

The children this year have been very well-behaved. It is something we've all noticed and commented on in the lounge. The women think it's me. I am the only man. I teach sixth grade and take most of the gym classes. I have the basketball team. The Safety Patrol is my responsibility.

It is crazy but I am in love with all of these women in the school. Miss A, Miss B, Miss C, Miss D, Miss E, Miss F, Miss G, Miss H, Miss I, Miss J, Miss K, and Miss L who teaches kindergarten. The principal, Miss M. The nurse, N, who visits twice a week, I first met during hearing tests this fall. The children were listening to earphones, curling and uncurling their index fingers in response to the pure tone. The music teacher, Miss O. The art instructor, Miss P.

How did I get here? It is difficult to say. But with each it seemed natural enough. Each relationship has a life of its own.

There is a lot of locker-room talk in the lounge and during staff meetings. When we meet in a group I'm ignored, taken for granted, as they search around inside their brown bags for the apple, rinse the flatware in the sink. They talk about their boyfriends. In all cases that would be me they are talking about. None knows of my other affairs. When they yak about love they do so casually so as not to let on to the others, to tease me with this our inside joke. Their candor protects them, renders me harmless; their wantonness deflects suspicion from the room.

It is exciting. I share a preparation time with Miss D. We smooch for the half-hour in the lounge. The coffee perks. Our red pens capped. On the playground Miss C chases me playfully, jogging, then sprinting. The children are playing tether ball, box ball. They're screaming. She always almost catches me. When children from our classes are in the lavatory, I hold hands for a second with Miss G as we lean against the yellow tile brick in the hall. She turns her body around, presses her face against the cool wall. I haven't been compromised, because none of them wants to be discovered. If I am alone with one, the others leave us alone because the only time any one of them wants to be with me is when she can be alone with me. I love the moment when we all step out in the hall, look at each other and step back in the classroom, drawing the door behind us to begin teaching that day.

SAFETY PATROL

I am the only man, but I don't think that has much to do with the discipline of the children. Perhaps there is something in the air. It's history, I think. I like teaching history, geography, health, the big wide books that contain all of the pictures. You know the old saying about history: study history or you're doomed to repeat it. That's all wrong, I think. You study it *and* you are doomed to repeat it. Maybe even more so because you study what's happened. Get to know it and it's like it's already happened. It is the same story over and over. It is time once again for kids to raise their hands, part their hair, say "please" and "thank you," follow directions. That's all.

❖

The Safety Patrol is in the rain. The streets are slick with oily rainbows, pooled. The gutters are full, flowing. The rain is soaking, steady. They are wearing bright yellow slickers. The water sheets down them. The bills of their yellow caps are pulled down flat between their eyes, hard against their noses like the gold helmets of heavy cavalry. The snaps are snapped beneath their chins. Their chins are tucked into their dryer chests. The flaps cover their ears, cheeks, necks. The claw fasteners shimmer down the fronts of their coats. They've polished them. They wear black rubber boots over their shoes. They stand in puddles, take the spray from passing cars without moving, their arms fixed at the proper angles, holding back the antsy students pressing to cross the streets into school.

The belts are orange, cinched tight over the shoulder, tight across the chest, over the heart, all buckled at the waist. The pools in the street turn red with the traffic light's light. The orange belts ignite as the headlights of the cars strike across them. For the instant it is just the belt floating without a body like the belt is bone in an X-ray.

The bells ring. We close the doors. Outside the patrol stays on the corners in case someone is tardy. Their heads pivot slowly checking all directions. Their faces sparkle. There are worms everywhere on the sidewalks. The towers' lights are juicy. Then from somewhere I can't see, I hear the clear call of the captain. "Off do tee." He calls again in the other direction, fainter. "Off do tee." Each syllable held a long time. Then the lieutenants at the far ends of the school repeat the same phrasing. The patrols leave the corners one by one, covering each other's moves as they all safely cross the wet streets and come into school.

❖

Each year I do a sociogram of my class. It helps me get a picture of how it all fits together, who the leaders are, who follow, who are lonely or lost, who are forgotten. I ask questions. Who in the class is your best friend, your worst enemy? Who is most like a sister, a brother? Who would you never tell a secret to? Who would you ask for help? Who is strongest? Who would you help? If a boy and a girl were drowning who would you save if you could only save one? Who would you give part of your lunch to? Who would you pick to be on your team in gym class? Who would you want to pick you? Who makes you laugh? Who makes you mad? If someone told you a secret and told you not to tell it to anyone in the class, who would you tell it to? Who do you miss during summer vacations? Who would you want to call you on the telephone? Who do you walk home with? Who would you walk home with if you could? If you could rename the school, who would you name it after? If you are a girl, which boy would you like to be just for a little while? If you are a boy, which girl would you like to be just for a little while? If something has to be done in class, who would you ask? Who would you want to do your homework? Who would you want to teach you a new game? Who ignores you? If you ran away, who would you send a letter to? If you were in the hospital, who would you want to see most? If you were afraid and by yourself in the dark, who would you call out for? The children like this test because they know the answers. They sneak looks at each other as they work. Their pencils wag.

I collect the data, assign values, note names. I graph responses, plot intersections. I never question their honesty. I can map out grudges and feuds, old loves, lingering feelings, all the tribal bonds and property disputes, the pecking order, the classes in the class.

And then I have conferences with the parents. We sit on the downsized chairs. I cast out the future for their son or daughter in the language of talk shows. I dissect the peer pressure, explain the forces at work. The parents want to know about change. Is this set in stone? Can my son be a leader, a professional? Will my daughter grow up to like men? I tell them that it's hard to say, that the children are all caught up in a vast machine of beliefs and of myths. It is of this group's own making. These responses are almost instinctual now, I tell the parents. Each class has its own history, its own biology, its own math and logic. I'm just presenting what's what.

I know now who leads the class and who operates in the shadows. I know where the power is and the anguish, who shakes down who, what favors are owed, who might turn a gun on his friends, on himself.

I ask these same questions of myself. I answer Miss A, Miss B, Miss C, Miss D, and so on. Who do I trust? Who would I save? Who would I want to go home with? I wish I could ask the women as well, but the results would be skewed.

There is no place to stand, no distance. Skewed.

❖

The Safety Patrol is in the hallway of the school before and after classes and at lunchtime. Inside, they wear the white cloth belts they launder. A bronze pin, given by the Chicago Motor Club, is attached where the belt begins to arch over the shoulder, the collar bone.

There is no running in the hall. The Patrol patrols up and down, one stationed every two or so classrooms. Stay on the right side of the hall. There is a red dashed line painted on the floor. The Patrol stands at ease, straddles the line. The small children move along cautiously, try not to look around. There is a bottle-neck near the piano on rollers that moves from classroom to classroom with the music teacher, Miss O. The piano is pushed keys first, against the wall. The bench is flipped on top of the upright. The legs point up like a cartoon of a dead animal. Handles are screwed on the side for easier moving. Something spills out of the intercom which only the teachers can understand. Loose squares of construction paper stapled on the bulletin boards lift and fall as kids pass by.

A Safety Patrol will speak. "What's your name?" and everyone in the hall will stop. "Yes, you," the Safety Patrol will say. Each member of the Safety Patrol can always see at least two other members. Their bright white belts cut across plaids and prints. They are never out of each other's sight.

They have arrayed themselves this way on their own, without my help. The captain and his lieutenants have posted schedules, worked out posts and their rotation. The Safety Patrol is on the corners of Tyler and State and on the corners of Tyler and Rosemount, and one is at the crossing on Stetler with the old crossing guard who has the stop sign he uses as a crook. A Patrol walks with a passel of kindergartners all the way to Spring Street, almost a mile, to push the button on the automatic signal. He eats his lunch on the corner and walks the afternoon students back to school. A lone Patrol guards the old railroad tracks that separate the school from Tower Heights. There are Patrols at each door into the building. They are strung through the halls. There, I've seen them straightening the reproductions of famous paintings the PTA has donated. They watch over the drinking fountains. They turn lights out in empty classrooms. They roust stragglers from the restrooms.

❖

I want my students to copy each other's work. It is a theory of mine. I've put the slower ones in desks right next to the ones who get it. I've told them that it is all right by me if they ask their neighbors for the answers, fine also for the neighbors to tell.

They want to know if they own their answers.

They want to know what happens if they don't want to tell.

Fair questions. I see them covering their papers with their hands and arms as they go along, turning their backs on the copier.

"What are you protecting?" I ask them. Students can't break the habits they have of cheating. They look out of the corners of their eyes. They whisper. They sneak. They drop pencils on the floor. They don't get this, my indifference. My indulgence. If they would ask me I would tell them the answers but it never occurs to them to ask me.

We are doing European Wars. The Peloponnesian. The Punic. The Sackings. The Hundred Years. The Thirty Years. We are studying an Eskimo girl and a boy from Hawaii. Our newest states. We are doing First Aid. We are doing the Solar System. We are doing New Math. We spell every Wednesday and Friday. We read "A Man without a Country."

We have taken a field trip to one of the television stations to appear on the "Engineer John Show," a show that airs in time for the kids coming home from school. Engineer John dresses like a railroad engineer — pin-stripe bib overalls, red neckerchief, crowned hat, a swan-necked oil can, big gloves. Really he is the other type of engineer who works with the transmitters, the wires, the towers, the kind in broadcasting, during the rest of the day. As a personality, he is cheap. He introduces Sergeant Preston movies and Hercules cartoons and short films provided by the AFL-CIO called *Industry on Parade,* which show milk bottles filling on assembly lines or toasters being screwed together. There are no people in the films. The students love the show, especially the factories of machines building other machines. They think Engineer John is a clown like Bozo, who is on another station, because they don't know what the costume means. To us in the studio audience he talked about electricity while the films ran on the monitors. He talked about the humming we heard.

Later, we wound through the neighborhood in a yellow bus dwarfed by the towers, dropping students at their houses. I sat in the back of the bus next to the emergency door with Miss J, holding her hand and rubbing her leg. We both looked straight ahead. Squeezed.

The Safety Patrol made sure the windows did not drop below the lines, that hands and heads and arms stayed inside. The captain whispered directions to the driver. The stop-sign arm extended every time we stopped. All the lights flashed as if we had won something.

❖

Every year there is a city-wide fire drill. All the schools, public and parochial, evacuated simultaneously. An insurance company provides red badges for the children, the smaller children wear fire hats. They are sent home with a checklist of hazards and explore their houses. Piles of rags and papers. Pennies in the fuse box. Paint cans near the water heater. I know they watch as their parents smoke. They inventory matches. They plan escapes from every room, crawl along floors. They touch doors quickly to see if they are hot before they open them. Extension cords. They set fire to their own pajamas.

In school they discuss their findings with each other, formed up in circles of chairs. They draw posters. They do skits.

On the day of the drill a fire company visited. Their pumper was in the parking lot gleaming. A radio station, WOWO, broadcast messages from the chief and the mayor and the superintendent. These were piped through to our classroom. A voice counted down the time to the moment when a little girl in a Lutheran elementary school this year would throw the switch and all the buzzers and bells in every other school would ring. Of course, this drill is never a surprise. That's not the point. Usually the alarm just sounds, and those assigned to close the windows close the windows. They turn out the lights. They leave everything. My students form into single file, are quiet for instructions, no shoving, no panic, know by heart where to go, what area of the playground to collect in, how to turn and watch the school, listen for the all-clear or the distant wail of sirens.

❖

I arrive at school in the dark. The Safety Patrol is already sowing salt along the sidewalks. Their belts quilt their heavy overcoats. They are scooping sand from the orange barrel that is stored at an angle in a wooden frame on the corner with the little hill. The captain watches over the dim streets as others spread the sand in sweeping arcs. Going by, the few cars crush the new snow. In the still air, I can clearly hear them chopping ice and shoveling the snow.

❖

I gave all the women sample-sized bottles of cheap perfume I bought at Woolworth's. Their desks were covered with tiny packages wrapped in color comics and aluminum foil, gifts from their students. I smelled the musky odor everywhere in the school for months later.

Miss J sent me a note one day. A fifth-grader, one size too small, handed it up to me. It was on lined notebook paper. Three of the five holes ruptured when she pulled it from the ringed notebook. In the beautiful blue penmanship many of the women have: *Do you like me? Yes or No.* She had drawn in little empty squares behind yes and no. The fifth-grader waited nervously just outside the door. My class in the middle of base two watched me as I filled in the *yes* square and folded up the paper. I sealed it with a foil star, sent the child back to the room. My own students watched me closely. I knew they were trying to guess the meaning of what I did.

I thought I saw them all blink at the same time. I couldn't be sure, because I can't see all the eyes at once, but it was a general impression, a feeling, a sense I had, a moment totally my own in my classroom when what I did was not observed.

In the lounge the smell of the perfume is strongest, overpowering the cool purple smell of mimeograph, the gray cigarette smoke, the green mint breath, the brown crushed smell of the wet Fort Howard paper towels.

Miss A has drawn our initials, big block printing, in her right palm, stitched together with a plus sign. Her hands are inscribed with whorls and stars, marks against cooties and answers to problems. If I just touch her she thrills and titters, runs and hides, rubbing her body all over with her streaked hands.

❖

In Fort Wayne we say there are more cars per capita than in any other city in the United States except Los Angeles. I believe it when I am caught in traffic on State Street. Up ahead are the school and the axle factory and a little beyond them the towers. We creep along one to a car through a neighborhood built after the war. All the houses have shutters with cutouts of sailboats or moons or pine trees.

I drive a Valiant. I shift gears by pushing buttons on the dash, an idea that didn't catch on.

In the middle of the intersection I am waiting to turn across the oncoming lane. The Safety Patrol watches me, knows my funny old car. It has no seat belts. The way they hold their hands, their heads, it's like a crucifixion. Their faces are fixed.

I am stopped again by the crossing guard in the street. He leans heavily on the striped dazzling pole. I have seen him swat the hoods of cars that have come too close. The Safety Patrol is behind him, funneling the children along the crosswalk of reflecting paint smeared in slashes on the street.

The guard has told me a story that may be true. He says when he was a boy he saw his kid brother die at the first traffic light in Fort Wayne. The light had no yellow, only the green and red flags snapping up and down. The boys knew what it meant, crossed with the light, but the driver came on through, peeled the one brother from the other. It was a time, the guard has said, when signs meant nothing.

He has played in the street. When he was a boy, he told me, he played in the street, Calhoun, Jefferson, highways now, throwing a baseball back and forth with his brother. They didn't have to move all day. He drove cattle down Main Street, cows home to be milked twice a day, then back out to pasture.

He remembers when all the land the school is on and all the land around was a golf course, and before that a swamp. All of this was a swamp, he says.

I like old things. I like the old times. It doesn't take long for things to get old. Everything seems to have been here all along but often it is not old.

Our principal tells us one day there will be no students, the neighborhood is aging, running out of babies, but there is no evidence of that. The school is teeming every year, spontaneous generation. We do that old experiment each year in the spring. The cheesecloth over the spoiled and the rotting meat grows its fur of maggots. The children love this.

Getting out of my car in the parking lot I am almost hit by something. It zips by my ear. Something skitters across the pavement. Nearby Miss F flings acorns my way, Brazils, cashews, mixed nuts. When we're alone she pinches me long and hard, won't let up, kicks me on the shins. She bites when we kiss. She says she likes me, she doesn't mean to hurt me. She wants me so much she wants to eat me up.

❖

This is an elementary school. The sprawling one-story was built in the 1950s with Indiana limestone, a flat roof, and panels in primary colors. Its silhouette is reminiscent of the superstructures of the last luxury liners — the SS *United States*, the *France* — streamlined with false ledges and gutters trailing off the leeward edges, giving the illusion of swift movement.

The Safety Patrol makes a big deal of raising and lowering the flag. Three or four members and always an officer parade out in the courtyard. There are salutes and an exaggerated hand-over-hand as the flag that flew over the nation's Capitol goes up and down. They fold the flag in the prescribed way, leaving, when done properly, that pastry of stars which one of them holds over his or her breast.

Finally, you can never be emotionally involved with any of this. That's a fact, not a warning.

This is an elementary school. The children move on. I have their homeroom assignments for junior high school. It's all alphabetical from now on. I come to the school believing it is some kind of sacred precinct. Teachers are fond of saying how much we learn from the children, how when we paddle it will hurt us more than it will hurt them. Tests test what? What was learned or how it was taught? Children are like any other phenomenon in nature.

The first steps in the scientific methods according to the book are to observe, collect data. An hypothesis would be an intimate act. All the experiments would be failures. I know my job. I am supposed to not know more than I do now. No research. I repeat each year the elemental knowledge I embody, the things I learned a long time ago.

I watch the seasons change on the bulletin boards. I take down the leaves for the turkeys and the pilgrims, and the leaves leave a shadow of their shapes burned into the yellow and orange and brown construction paper. The sun has faded the background.

The stencils and straight pins, colored tacks and yarns, the cotton-ball snow, the folded doily flakes, no two alike. The eggshell flowers are in the spring. The grass cut into a fringe on a strip of green paper is curled bluntly through the scissors. The summer is cork.

❖

The Safety Patrol folds its belts like flags. At the end of the school day they are sitting at their desks folding their belts to store them away. The other children have already been ferried across the streets. It is like a puzzle or trying to fold a map. The trick is to master the funny angle of the crossing belt, the adjusting slides, the heavy buckle. It's like folding parachutes. They leave the packets in the center of their desktops, the bronze pin on top of each.

I go home and watch the "Engineer John Show." There are so many kinds of people that exist now only on TV — milkmen, nuns in habit, people who live in lighthouses, newsboys who yell "Extra." Engineer John arrives with the sound of a steam engine.

We know that when tornadoes happen they are supposed to sound like freight trains. It is spring and the season for tornadoes, which Fort Wayne is never supposed to have according to an old Indian belief, still repeated, that the three rivers ward them off. We will drill. The students sit Indian-fashion under their desks, backs to the windows. Or in the hall the bigger children cover their smaller brothers and sisters.

During our visit, Engineer John told us about the ground. How electricity goes back to it, finds it. I thought of the towers as a type of well. These pictures gushing from the field, a rich deposit. The electrons pump up and down the shafts.

In storms, the children say they watch the lightning hit the towers. They turn their sets off and watch. The towers are sometimes up inside the clouds. The clouds light up like lampshades. I think a lot of people watch the towers, know which windows in their houses face that way. They sit up and watch when the storm keeps them awake. Or when they can't sleep in general, maybe they stare out at all the soothing, all the warning lights.

The sixth-grade girls are gathered in one room to watch the movie even I have never seen. I have the boys. They are looking up words in the dictionary. I tell them that dictionaries have very little to do with spelling but with history, with where the word comes from, how long it has been used and understood.

Miss K calls me out in the hall. The doors are closed and she leads me to the nearest girls' restroom and pulls me inside. I always feel funny in the wrong washroom, hate to open the door even to yell in "Hurry up" to my girls, who are just beginning to use makeup and are dawdling over the sinks and mirrors.

We cram into the furthest stall, and Miss K unbuttons her dress, which has her initials embroidered on her dollar — AMR. We have played doctor before in the nurse's room, where there are screens, couches and gowns. There are even some cold metal instruments ready on a towel. She is in her underwear when we hear the doors wheeze, and someone comes in. A far stall door clicks closed and we hear the rustle of clothes and the tinkle. Miss K worms around me, crouches down to look beneath the partition. Elastic snaps. The flush. We hear hands being washed in the sink, dried on paper towels.

When we're alone again Miss K finishes undressing. She clutches pieces of her clothes in each hand, covers her body and then quickly opens her arm. She lets me look at her, turns around lifting her hands over her head, clothes spilling down, taking rapid tiny steps in place. She tucks her clothes into the wedge of her elbows, hugging the bundle next to her breast, her bronze nipple. She reaches down between her legs with her other hand, watching me as she does so, trying not to giggle. Then she shows me her hand. There is some blood on her fingers, she thinks it is so funny. She couldn't sit through the movie.

Perhaps all of the women in the school are bleeding at the same moment, at this moment, by chance or accident, through sympathy, gravity, vibration. It's possible. It could be triggered by suggestion, by a school year of living out blocks of time, periods of periods, drinking the same water, breathing the same air. And what if it had happened, is happening? Would it be any worse if the planets all aligned or if everyone in the world jumped up in the air at the same time? The school, a little worse for wear a few days each month, tense, cramped, even horny, a word my students always giggle at. And now that some of them are alone with dictionaries I know they are looking up all the words they've never said and know they should never say.

❖

The bright yellow tractors are back cutting the grass around the school. The litter in the lawn is mulched and shot out the side with the clippings. The driver takes roughly a square pattern, conforming to the shape of the lawn, the patches fitting inside each other. The green stripe is a different shade depending upon the angle of the light — flat green, the window of cut grass and the bright lush grass still standing. The tractors emit those bleating sounds when they back up, trimming around trees.

I see all of this through my wall of windows. The Safety Patrol on their corners cover their ears as the tractors come near. I can see them shouting to the other children, waving at them, yanking them around. Their voices lost in the roar of the mowers. They mean to take the shrapnel of shredded branches, stones, crushed brick, the needles of grass into their own bodies. An heroic gesture they must have learned from television.

❖

The word *carnival* means "the putting away of flesh," according to *The American Heritage Dictionary*. I feel as if no one knows this as I thread through the crowded school halls.

Parents and neighbors and high-school kids have come to the carnival. We're just trying to raise money for audio-visual equipment, tumbling apparati, maybe buy a few more trees. The students are here, many with their faces painted like clowns, one of the attractions. Some fifth-graders are following me around since they have learned I'll be their teacher next year. They're drinking drinks that a fast-food place donates. Their lips and tongues are orange or purple or red or a combination of those colors. Underfoot a carpet of popcorn pops where we walk. The floors are papered with discarded spin art and scissored silhouettes. People are wearing lighter clothes, brighter clothes. They form clots in the hall, push and shove. Children are crying or waving long strips of the blue tickets above their heads, hitting others as they go by. It is a job, this having fun.

Each room has a different game run by the teachers and room mothers. I am floating from one place to the other, bringing messages and change, tickets and cheap prizes. One room has the fish pond. I see the outline of Miss B working furiously behind the white sheet, attaching prizes to the hooks. Children are on the other side of the sheet holding long tapering bamboo poles. In another room is the candy wheel. Another has a plastic pool filled with water and identical plastic ducks. There are rooms where balls are tossed at hoops and silver bottles. There is the cakewalk. One room is even a nursery where mothers are nursing or changing their babies. In all the rooms are the cards of letters — Aa Bb Cc Dd Ee, some in cursive Aa Bb Cc Dd Ee with tiny arrows indicating the stroke of the pen. There are green blackboards, cloakrooms, the same clock, the drinking fountain and the illuminated exit sign over the door.

In the cafetorium adults are having coffee. Children are rolling in the mats. Pigs in blankets are being served, beans, Jell-O. Up on the stage behind the heavy curtains is the Spook House. Four tickets. There is a long line.

In the dark you are made to stumble and fall. Strings and crepe streamers propelled by fans whip your face. There are tugs on your clothes, your shoes, your fingers. There are noises, growls, shrieks, laughs. Things are revealed to you, such as heads in boxes, spiders, skulls, chattering teeth. All the time you can hear the muttering of the picnic outside damped by the curtain, the thrumming of conversation. And your eyes just get used to the dark when you come upon a table set with plates each labeled clearly: Eyeballs, Fingers, Guts, Hearts, Blood, Brains. You can see clearly now the cocktail onions, the chocolate pudding, the ketchup, the Tootsie Rolls, the rice, everything edible. The tongue, tongue. Someone is whispering over and over "touch it, touch it." And it's hard to, even though you know what these things really are. Or you want to because you know you never would touch the real things.

THE SAFETY PATROL 127

I go outside up on the roof, I have the key, to sneak a smoke. The Safety Patrol is out in the parking lot. The towers are sputtering off in the distance. For a couple of tickets you take a couple swings with a sledge hammer at an old car. The car looks very much like mine.

The glass is all removed, the sharp edges. It only looks dangerous. The sound reaches me a heartbeat after I see the hammer come down. People like the thin metal of the roof, the hood and trunk, the fine work around the head and taillights. The grill splinters. The door that covers the gas cap is a favorite target.

The Safety Patrol rings the crumpled car, holding back the watching crowd a prudent distance. Their belts together are a kind of hound's-tooth pattern. In the moonlight the metal of the car shines through the dented enamel and catches fire. The car has been spray-painted with dares and taunts. A blow takes the hammer through the door, and there is chanting. Again. Again. Again. And the Safety Patrol joins hands.

Michael Martone's first book of stories, *Alive and Dead in Indiana,* was published in 1984. For the last seven years, Martone lived in Story County, Iowa, where he and his wife, Theresa Pappas, published Story County Books. He now lives in Massachusetts.

Safety Patrol

Designed by Chris L. Smith.
Composed by Capitol Communications, Inc., in English Times with
    display lines in Belwe Light.
Printed by The Maple Press Company on 50-lb. Antique Cream,
    bound in Kivar 5 and Papan with Multicolor Antique endsheets,
    and stamped in red and black.